JUST WACKY!

Is this the right book for you?
Take the WACKY TEST and find out.

YES	NO	
☐	☐	Do you bounce on your bed so high that your head hits the ceiling?
☐	☐	Do you ever look in the mirror and see a wide-eyed lunatic grinning back at you?
☐	☐	Do you sometimes get the urge to take off your clothes and cover yourself in mud?
☐	☐	Do you often waste your time taking crazy tests like this one?

SCORE: Give yourself one point for each YES answer.

3–4   You are completely wacky.
       You will love this book.

1–2   You are not completely wacky.
       You will love this book.

0   You are so wacky, you don't even
       realize you're wacky.
       You will love this book.

Also by Andy Griffiths

Just Annoying!
Just Joking!
Just Stupid!
The Day My Butt Went Psycho!
Zombie Butts from Uranus!

ANDY GRIFFITHS

JUST Wacky!

with illustrations by... TERRY DENTON

Scholastic Inc.

New York   Toronto   London   Auckland   Sydney
Mexico City   New Delhi   Hong Kong   Buenos Aires

ISBN 0-439-42473-9

12   11   10   9   8   7   6   5   4   3   2   1   4   5   6   7   8   9/0

Printed in the U.S.A.   40
First Scholastic printing, October 2004

JUST Wacky!

CONTENTS

JUST Wacky!

APART FROM MY PRESENCE,
EXPLAINING MY PRESENCE,
THIS PAGE IS ENTIRELY
   B L A N K.
ALTHOUGH THERE IS A LOT
OF STUFF OUTSIDE THE
EDGES OF THE PAGE THAT
I CANNOT REALLY SHARE WITH
YOU, BECAUSE YOU CANNOT SEE
IT. BUT I CAN. AND I'M ONLY AN
OLD CHICKEN BONE. YOU MUST
FEEL A BIT STUPID, BEING BETTERED
BY AN OLD CHICKEN BONE. EH!

Band-Aid

Have you ever had a Band-Aid on for so long that you can't tell where the Band-Aid ends and your skin begins?

I have.

In fact, I have one on right now.

It's been on for the last six months.

I've grown quite attached to it actually, and it's grown quite attached to me.

We've spent a lot of time together.

WHO WOULD EVER HAVE THOUGHT THAT THIS OL' BONE WOULD ONE DAY END UP OWNING HIS OWN BAND-AID. WOW!

I did some calculations and I figured that I've had the Band-Aid on for one hundred and eighty-two and a half days, which is four thousand three hundred and eighty hours, or two hundred and sixty-two thousand and eight hundred minutes, or fifteen million seven hundred and sixty-eight thousand seconds, or even more precise, well, I can't be any more precise because my calculator conked out when I tried to figure out how many milliseconds. There wasn't enough room on the screen for all the zeroes.

But you don't need to know how many milliseconds it is to know that it's more than enough time for a Band-Aid to get a very serious grip.

It's not my fault I had to leave it on so long. It's Mom's fault.

If she didn't act like Band-Aids cost about three million dollars each, I'd be able to change them more often. She hides them, and if I get hurt — no matter how bad — she'll only let me have one Band-Aid, and that's it.

ME? A BAND-AID? NO, MADAM. YOU MUST HAVE ME CONFUSED WITH SOMEONE ELSE. I AM A TOURIST.

If I pull it off too soon and ask her for another one, she says, "Do you think we're made of Band-Aids? Do you think Band-Aids grow on trees? Do you think Band-Aids are handed out free on street corners?" And it doesn't matter how many times I ask her, she won't give me another one. So I've learned to leave them on. But I think I've left this one on just a little bit too long.

I'm never going to get it off.

But I have to.

2

Welcome!

Because we've got school photos today.

And it's on my face. Right under my left eye.

I can't have my photo taken with a Band-Aid on my face.

I'll look like an idiot.

I'll look even stupider than the year I blinked.

And even more stupider than the year the bench I was standing on rocked unexpectedly, and I opened my mouth in surprise.

If I have my picture taken with this Band-Aid on, everybody will look at the photograph when they're older and they won't remember me as the brilliant genius I was — they'll just remember me as the idiot with the Band-Aid on his face.

It's not fair.

I always get Band-Aids.

Everybody else has these really cool accidents where they end up with their arms and legs in a cast and they get all the sympathy and attention and everybody wants to sign their casts — it makes me sick. Why can't I get a really good injury like that? It would be so cool to break every bone in my body and have to go to the hospital and just lie around and watch television and eat ice cream all day long.

But that will never happen to me.

If I broke every bone in my body, the doctor would just look at me and say, "He'll be all right. Just put a couple of Band-Aids on him." And then my mom would look at the doctor with her hands on her hips and say, "*Two* Band-Aids? Do you think I'm made of Band-Aids? Do you think Band-Aids grow on trees? Do you think Band-Aids are handed out free on street corners?" And the doctor would say, "Actually, you're right — one Band-Aid will be adequate."

Anyway, that's pretty much the story of my life when it comes to accidents. Nothing too serious. Not even the latest accident, which *should* have been a lot more serious than it actually was.

I found this pair of glasses on the way home from school. Little gold-rimmed spectacles, just lying in the middle of the sidewalk.

I would have left them there except I'd read a survey in the paper saying that most people thought people who wore glasses were more intelligent than people who didn't wear them. So I had this idea that maybe I could make my teachers think that I'm smarter than I really am, and they would give me better grades. So I picked up the glasses and put them on, but the

JUST SERIOUS ACCIDENTS: Nº 36.

FALLING OFF TALL TOWER INTO DRINK BOTTLE.

4

ME, MECHANICAL BIRD.

lenses made everything sort of shaky and out of focus. The last thing I heard before I fell was, "Look out!"

I ended up at the bottom of a roadworkers' ditch.

But did I get a broken leg?

No.

A broken arm?

No.

Massive head injuries, complex fractures, amnesia, and a nasty bruise?

No.

The only thing that broke were the glasses, and the only injury I got was a cut under my left eye.

So much for glasses making you look more intelligent. I ended up looking stupider than ever.

But I'll fix that.

This Band-Aid has got to go.

And today is the day.

I can't put it off any longer.

I grit my teeth.

I clench my jaw.

I take a deep breath.

This is it.

Stinging.

HANDY
RECIPES:
NO. 6.
BAND-AID
MUFFINS.
FLOUR.
EGGS.
MILK.
SUGAR.
...ETC...
YUM!

5

YOU, READER.

REMOVING A
BAND-AID
WITH NASA's
HELP.

Burning.

Agony.

Pure agony.

More pure agony.

And I haven't even started yet.

Just thinking about it is painful.

What if my skin comes off with it?

What if I start to bleed and I can't stop?

And what if I just bleed and bleed and bleed, and the whole bathroom fills up with blood?

And what if I'm just treading blood and then my mom opens the door and all the blood surges out of the room like a tidal wave and picks Mom up as well as me and we go sailing off down the street, and Mom screams, "What's happening?" and I'll say, "I just peeled off my Band-Aid, that's all," and she'll say, "What? You peeled your Band-Aid off? Do you think I'm made of Band-Aids? Do you think Band-Aids grow on trees? Do you think Band-Aids are handed out free on street corners?" And I'll say, "No, but they should be because then I wouldn't have had to wear the same one for six months and none of this would have ever happened!"

But you can go crazy thinking about stuff like this.

Better not to think about it.

I know what I should do.

Stop thinking and just do it.

Fast.

Get it over and done with.

A lot of people prolong the agony by thinking about it too much.

But not me.

When I say I'm going to do something, then I do it. I don't just go on and on about it. I do it.

Really.

I really, really do it. Here goes.

I'm going to do it.

Right now.

Starting in a moment.

A moment from right now.

I mean right then.

Because in the time it took me to think this, right now became right then. And in the time it took me to think how right now became right then, right then became even righter then. And I can't start righter then because that's already gone so I'm going to start right now instead.

On the count of three.

One. Two. Two and a half. Two and three-quarters. Two and four-fifths. Two and five-

TRY IT YOURSELF.

MECHO NOT HAPPY.

sixths. Two and six-sevenths. Two and seven-eighths . . .

This is not really working.

Better not to count.

Better just to do it.

Better to stop talking about it and thinking about it and just do it. Do it. Really do it.

Now!

REMOVING A BAND-AID IN ANCIENT TIMES.

But first I need a pair of tweezers because the edge of the Band-Aid is so gummed down that there's nothing for me to grab onto.

I open the bathroom cabinet and look around inside it for the tweezers. I can't believe the stuff that's in here.

Baby shampoo, apple shampoo, anti-dandruff shampoo (that's Dad's in case you're wondering), barrettes, razor blades, a jar of antiwrinkle cream (that's Mom's), sunscreen, Q-Tips, pimple cream (that's Jen's — although if you ask me, it's not working; in fact, I think it's having the opposite effect), headache pills, vitamin C tablets, worming tablets (they're Sooty's . . . I think), a little container of weird-smelling ointment that Dad sometimes rubs on his toes, about ten rolled-up tubes of almost-but-not-quite-finished toothpaste . . . practically everything in the world except tweezers.

1,000 lbs.

SKLITCH!! 8 NEED LEG.

And if you think I'm stalling for time by listing every single thing that's in the bathroom cabinet, then you're wrong. I haven't even mentioned the perfume, the mouthwash — Jen's, of course — the lip balm, the bottles of nail polish, or the lipsticks. I could have mentioned these things but I didn't because I'm not trying to waste time. . . . I'm just trying to find the tweezers.

I open the first aid kit.

Ah! There they are.

I take them out.

Now I can get this Band-Aid off, once and for all.

Except that the tweezers are a little dirty. I should sterilize them under some hot water. You can't be too careful where germs are concerned.

I rinse the tweezers under the hot water faucet.

I suppose you think I'm stalling again. Well, I'm not.

I'm not scared of a little pain.

In fact, I like it.

I thrive on it.

As far as I'm concerned, the more pain the better!

THE SAD STORY OF MRS. TWEEZERS

20 YEARS LATER.

TWEEZER SKELETON.

SPLUTCH.

REMOVING
A BAND-AID
BY PIANO.

Sometimes, when I'm hammering a nail into a piece of wood, I like to hit my thumb on purpose — just to feel it throb. When I'm handling paper, I always try to get a paper cut because they *really* hurt. And I always make sure I lick my knife because tongue cuts are even more painful than paper cuts. But if you think that's bad, that's nothing. I've got a book called *The Encyclopedia of Executions,* and there's some stuff in there that's a lot worse than that. Like, for instance, there's people getting boiled alive, burned at the stake, and stretched out in the desert, covered with honey and eaten by ants. . . . But all that is nothing compared to the pain of peeling off a Band-Aid that's been stuck to your skin for six months.

But it must be done.

And it's going to be done now.

The tweezers are ready.

I turn off the faucet.

I brace myself.

I slide the points of the tweezers under the gummy edge of the Band-Aid and start pulling . . . AAAAAAAGGGGGGGGHHHH-HHH!!! @%*!!!!!!!@ @##**@ OUCH!! $!$%#% #$% @@ EEEEEEEK!! #!!!!*!!!!! !!@@##**@ # YOW!! %&^%# #@!!!#@# $!$%#%#$%@ @#

1,000 lbs.

10

ARM NOT FUNNY.

!!!!*!!!!!!!@ @##**@#!%&^%# #@!!!#@#$!$ %#
%#$%@@#!!!! *!!!!!!!@ @##**@# AAAGGGG-
HHH!!! %&^%###@!!!# @#$!$%#%# $%@
@#!!!!*!!!!! !!@@##**@#!%&^%# #@!!!#@#$!$
%#%#$% GRRRRRR!!! M@@#!!!!*!!! !!!!@@
##**@#!%&^%# #@!!!#@#$!$ OOOCH! %#%
#$%@@ #!!!!*!!!!!! !@@##** @#!%&^%## @!!!#
OUOIU!!!! @# $!$%#%#$%@@ #!!!!* !!!!!!!@@#*
*@#!%&^%##@!! !#@#$!$%#% UGGGH!!!! #$
%@@#!!!!*! !!!!!!@@##** @#!%&^%## @!!!#@#
$!$%#%#%#KHKJHOH!!!! $%@ @#!!!!*!!!!!!!@ @#
#**@#!%&^%# #@!!! #@# $!$%#%#$ %@@#
!!!!*!! !!!!!@ @##* OUCH!!! *@#!% &^ %##@!!!
#@#$!$%#%#$ %@@#!!!!*!! !!!!!@@##**@ #!
%&^ %##@!!! #@# $!$%#%#$ %@@#!!!!*!!!
OWWWW!!!! @@##**@#!%&^ %# RESTRS-
GFS!!!! #@!!!# @#$! $%#%#$%@@#!!!!*!!!! !!!
@@##**@# !%&^%##@!!!# @#$!$%#%#$%@ @
#!!!!* !!!!!!!@@##**@#!%& EEEEEK!!! ^%##
@!!! #@ #$!$%#%#$YOWWWWW!!! %@@#
!!!!*!!!!!!! @@ ##**@#!%&^%##@!!!#@ #$!$%
#%# $%@@#!!!!* !!!!!!!@@# #**@#!%&^%##
GFFGNEYTHGNS{A!!! @!!!#@#$!$ %#%#$ %
@@ #!!!!*!!!!!!! @##**@# ZXCZXZCV!!!! % &^
%##@!! @#$!$%#% #$%@@#!!!!* !!!!!!@@ ##**
#!%&^PLKDVVVV!!! ##@!!!# @#$!$%# %#$%
@@#!!!!*!!!!!!!@@##**@#!%&^%##@ !!!#@ #$!$

TTKLMNX
OPQ STR N.

T.

PNWX B
O TNKTB

RSPNTOK?
OWNTK, LB
TWXOKN!!!

11

KLZSMPK!
OONZKT.

NKLP
TTWN.

%#%#$%@ @#!!!!*!!!!!!! @IAARR? I?I?!!! @## **@#!% &^%##@!!!#@ #$!$%#% #$%@@#!!!! *!!!!!!!@@ OWWWW !!!##**@#! %& ^%##@!! !#@#$!$%#%#$%@@#!!!!*!!!!!!! @@ ##**@#!%& ^%##@!!!#@#$! $%#%#$ AAAGHHH %@@#!!!! *!!!! !!!@@## MMMNNBNBHHVG!!! **@#!% &^% ##@ !!!#@#$!$% #%#$% @@#!!!!*!!!!!!! @@##**@#!%&^QWSQWQSWS!!!! %## @!!!#@# $!$%#%#$%@@ #!!!!*!!!!!! @@##**@#! %&^% ##@!!!#@#$!$%# %#$%@@#!!!!*!!! !!!@@##* *@ #!%&^%##@!!! #@#$!$%#%# AAAGGH $%@@ #!!!!*!!!!!!! !@@##**@#!%& AAGGHHH!!!! %## @!!!#@ #$!$%# %#$%@@ #!!!!*!!!!!!!@ @##** @#!%&^ %##@!!!#@#$!$%#%#M.ZSVKHGDC; WKC AJG!!!! $%@@# !!!!*!!!!!!!@@##**@#!%& ^%## @!!!#@ #$!$%#%#%$%@@#!!!!*!!!!!!! @@##** @#!%&^%##@ YIKES!!! #@#$!% #%# $%@@ #!!!!*!!!!!!!@@ ##* * SDFACAVCA!!! @# !%&^% ##@ !!!#@# $!$%# %#$%@@#!!!!*!!!!!!! @@## **@#!%& ^%X WRTUIYLKTYUJRE!!!!#@ !!!#@ HUKLOLOIKM!!!! #$!$%#%#$%@@ #!!!! *!!! !!!!@ @##**@#!% &^%##@!!!#@#$! $%# %#$ %@ @#!!!!*!!!!!!!@@##**@#!%&^%## OOOOHHHH!!! #@#$!$% #%#$%@@#!!!!* !!! !!!!@@ ##**@#!%&^%## @!!!#@#$!$%#%# $% @@ #!!!!*!!!!!!!@@##**@#!%&^%##@!!!#@ WOOHHH! #$!$%#%#$% @@#!!!!*!!!!!!!@ KFG

AZKLLPTW
OO BPTLK
NFL: 2G.

1,000 lbs.

12

SXKCHDGH!!! @ ##**@#!%& &^%##@!!! #@#
$!$%#%# $%@@ #!!!!*!!!!! !!@@DLKOKIHJY
HU!!! ##**@#!%&^ %##@!!!#@#$!$%# %#$%@
@#!!!!*!!!!!!!@@# #**@#!%&^% XXXXXCVBN
M,NVCB!!##@!!!#!#$!$%# %#$%@@#!!!!*!!!!!!!
@@## ** PIWEYRGPQWYHCI!!!!@#!%&^%##
@@!!!#@#$!$%#%# QEPIOURGHFP0WUY-
OUFJWPOFYVGOEUIDQERQWPEI7FTYN'!!!!
$%*$^*%$*^$ SD;UB,JXVFXFDJDFSKDSU!!!!
IDFLKDCGDNSDFXCZO!!!! IWRQOAXM,C;
VBJHH!!!! *!!!! !! !@@##**@#!% &^%##@!!!#@#
$!$%#% #$%@ @#!!!!* !!!!!!!@@ ##**@#!%&
^%##@!!! #@#$!$%# %#$%@ @#!!!! AAAGGGH-
HHH!!!

I have to stop.

It's the worst pain ever.

It's the worst pain in the history of worst pains.

And I've only peeled off a tiny fraction. I've still got another sixty-eight and a half fractions to go.

Maybe fast is not the answer.

But neither is slow.

I can't leave it on.

But I can't peel it off.

To peel or not to peel?

That is the question.

To PEEL OR NOT TO PEEL?

Or is it?

There must be a better way than peeling.

Peeling sucks.

It really sucks.

Sucks?

Sucks!

That's it!

Sucking is the answer!

I can use our new vacuum cleaner to suck this stupid Band-Aid off.

Our old vacuum cleaner broke recently and Mom and Dad replaced it with a new superpowerful model. It's so powerful that it can practically suck dust off the surface of the moon. Not that I've actually tried yet, but I bet it could.

The Band-Aid won't stand a chance.

All I'll have to do is wave the vacuum cleaner near it and the Band-Aid will be off in a second.

No peeling.

No pain.

No nothing.

Just one quick suck, and it will all be over.

I go to the hall closet and get the vacuum cleaner.

HUMBLE BAND-AIDS BOW DOWN IN HOMAGE BEFORE THE VISION OF THE SACRED SCAB.

1,000 lbs.

MECHO LOSE LEG.

14

It's huge. I drag it into the bathroom and plug it in.

I take the brush off the end of the nozzle. I don't want anything getting in the way of its sucking power.

I switch it on. The noise is incredible. It sounds like it's powered by a jet engine.

I'd better concentrate.

It's a tricky job because I have to use the mirror to guide the nozzle into position. And the nozzle is so long I can't get as close to the mirror as I'd like to.

I guide the nozzle close to the Band-Aid. I can feel the Band-Aid lifting, but not quite separating from my cheek.

I get a little closer.

Still not working.

I can't understand it. I should have pulled the Band-Aid free by now.

Maybe there's something blocking the nozzle. I pull it away from the Band-Aid and look into the end. But I can't see anything. It's too dark.

I put it up closer to my eye.

And closer.

And just a little bit closer.

HAND COVER PAGE NUMBER

FOR MORE INTERESTING FACTS ABOUT POWERFUL VACUUMS, TURN TO PG. 96

PHOOMPH!

My eye!

Help! The vacuum cleaner is stuck on my eye!

It's sucking my eyeball out of its socket!

The pain is incredible.

It's worse than paper cuts, tongue cuts, and whacking your thumb with a hammer all put together.

It's got to be even worse than being boiled alive, burned at the stake, or being stretched out in the desert, covered with honey and eaten by ants.

It's even worse than peeling off a Band-Aid . . . well . . . maybe not quite that bad, but you know what I mean.

And it's not just painful . . . it's potentially fatal.

It could suck my eyeball right out of its socket.

And my eyeball is connected to my brain. It could suck that out as well.

Which would be even worse because my brain is connected to everything else. . . . Any moment now, the whole inside of my body could be sucked out of my head!

I have to act.

HOW THE BODY WORKS: PART: 7

EYEBROWS AND EYEBALLS

BRAIN

1,000 lbs.

IS PAGE 16

Fast.

Now.

Right now!

I stretch out my leg and kick the OFF switch.

The noise dies down.

I pull the nozzle away from my eye and sit down on the side of the bathtub to catch my breath.

Right. That's it. Enough fooling around.

The vacuum cleaner is not the solution.

The Band-Aid is stuck on too well.

I'm just going to have to do it by hand.

I grab the Band-Aid in the middle, pinch it as hard as I can, and rip.

There.

It's off.

That wasn't so bad.

Hardly hurt a bit.

The trick to these things is just to get them over and done with as fast as possible.

I put the Band-Aid into my pocket — that could come in handy for annoying Jen later on. She hates used Band-Aids. She thinks they're disgusting. Especially when they turn up in her sandwiches.

I stand up and look in the mirror.

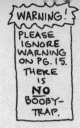

WARNING!
PLEASE IGNORE WARNING ON PG. 15. THERE IS NO BOOBY-TRAP.

WHERE TO HIDE A USED BAND-AID.

DRINK

BAKED POTATO

TOOTHBRUSH

PLUS ONE IS 18

It's amazing. Six months — and all that's left is a faint pink rectangle with a sticky gray outline.

No scar. Nothing. Just skin. Normal, perfectly healed skin.

Oh no.

I don't believe it.

The Band-Aid is gone and my cut has healed, but now I have a big red-and-black nozzle ring around my left eye. It's sort of a combination of a bruise and a blood blister.

I can't have my photo taken like this.

What am I going to do?

Now I won't look like an idiot with a Band-Aid under my eye — now I'll look like an idiot wearing half a pair of glasses.

Glasses.

Glasses!

What better way to get my photo taken? Everybody will look at the school photo and think, *Who's that intelligent-looking guy with the glasses? He must be sooooo smart*.

But I'm only wearing *half* a pair of glasses.

I need to finish the job.

I know what I have to do.

It's going to hurt, but it will be worth it.

THEN COME PAGE 22.

Like I said, I'm not scared of a little bit of pain.

I turn the vacuum cleaner back on.

It roars into action.

I put the nozzle up to my right eye.

Here goes.

PHOOMPH!

The nozzle grabs hold of my eyeball and starts sucking.

It doesn't feel quite as bad this time because I'm used to it, but still, it doesn't tickle.

WHAT THE EYE SEES LOOKING UP A SUCKING VACUUM.

WHAT THE VACUUM SEES.

I leave it there for as long as I can stand the pain. That should do it.

I turn around to hit the OFF switch, but as I do, the vacuum cleaner hose crashes into the open bathroom cabinet and wipes everything off the shelf.

It all comes tumbling off the shelves and smashes onto the bathroom tiles.

There's broken glass and shampoo and razor blades and perfume and soap and pills and foul-smelling ointment all over the floor. And the vacuum cleaner nozzle is still stuck on my eye. It's really starting to hurt now.

"BEWARE!" SAYS MS. PATERSON OF VICTIMS OF VACUUMS.

I go for the switch again, but as I do, I slip. I grab at the towel rack, but all I get is a towel. It slides off and I fall down, hard.

ME SICK OF THIS.

OOF!

The right side of my face crunches against the tiles. I hit something sharp.

OUCH!

I lift my head.

I see a razor blade.

I see blood.

Blood!

My blood is on the floor!

And the vacuum cleaner is sucking my eyeball out.

I try to stand up, but I can't. My ankle hurts too much.

I can't reach the switch.

I'm pulling at the vacuum cleaner nozzle with both hands, pulling as hard as I can but I can't get it off.

I'm too weak.

I'm losing too much blood.

What a crazy way to die!

I drag myself across the floor toward the vacuum cleaner.

I push the OFF switch.

The roaring subsides. The vacuum cleaner stops sucking.

I hold on to the sink and pull myself up.

I look in the mirror.

Oh no.

This is bad.

I have a big red-and-black nozzle mark around my right eye — it matches the other one perfectly. I look more intelligent than I ever dreamed possible.

But what I also have is a razor blade cut — just under my right eye.

It's bleeding.

A lot.

I'm going to need a Band-Aid on that.

A DOT
ON THE
PAGE.

A HOLE IN
THE PAGE
WITH AN
EYE
LOOKING
THROUGH.

21

YUM!
HAND
TASTE GOOD.

THE DOG ATE IT

Quick!" I yell. "We have to stop him!"

Danny and I are chasing Sooty down the hall.

He's just eaten the model flying saucer that we made for our assignment on aliens. There's nothing left except a few scraps of chewed cardboard.

It took us the whole weekend to make that. We made it out of paper plates, egg cartons, and toilet paper rolls. It was painted green and had these little aliens sitting in the cockpit we cut out from an egg carton. Well, they weren't really aliens — they were two of Danny's toy soldiers, but we melted their heads to make them look like aliens. It wasn't easy, either. We destroyed the whole platoon before we got two that looked exactly right. The flying saucer looked great, too — just like the real thing. We just left it for a moment and then Sooty went and ate it. I'm going to kill him.

Once I catch him.

He runs into the living room and scrambles under the couch.

"Get out!" I yell. "Get out right now!"

But Sooty is not stupid.

Dumb, but not stupid.

He stays under the couch. He knows how angry I am.

"Ms. Livingstone's going to be mad," I say.

"I know," says Danny. "We're going to have to make it all over again."

"We might be able to make another flying saucer," I say, "but we can't make any more aliens. We don't have any soldiers left, remember? You wrecked them all."

"*I* wrecked them all?" says Danny. "You were the one who had the blowtorch up too high."

"Yeah, well, whatever," I say. "The fact is that we don't have our assignment."

Danny shrugs. "We'll just tell Ms. Livingstone that Sooty ate it," he says.

"What?" I say. "Tell her the dog ate it?"

"Yeah," says Danny. "Why not?"

RAFF RAFF
SCAMPER LOVES TO EAT BROOMS.

TRIXI LOVES TO HIDE IN THE FISH BOWL.

WOOF.
MY DOG FIFI LIKES TO PLAY IN THE HOT WATER FAUCET.

"Are you kidding?" I say.

"But it's the truth," says Danny.

I shake my head.

"Danny," I say, "I know that and you know that, but to Ms. Livingstone, it will just sound like the most pathetic excuse in the world. Everybody uses that one!"

I'm not like Danny. I pride myself on my excuses. I may not get my homework in on time and I may not get the best marks, but I always have a good excuse. One that is original, brilliant, and most important, believable.

"Yeah," says Danny. "We need a really good excuse." He thinks for a moment. "How about we tell her your house burned down?"

"No good," I say. "I used that one a few months ago. Ms. Livingstone already thinks we're living in a tent while the house is being rebuilt."

"Why don't we tell her that the tent burned down?"

"Danny!" I say. "Get real."

Danny frowns and shrugs.

"I don't know," he says. "Why would Sooty eat our flying saucer, anyway? It was just cardboard and glue."

"He'll eat anything," I say. "Horse poo, dead

24

birds . . . you name it, he's eaten it. He even eats his own spew."

"Gross!" says Danny.

"Not to him," I say. "He loves it. Sometimes I think he vomits just so he can eat it again."

SOOTY'S STOMACH.

WE ARE IN A NEW WORLD, VO5.

JA, MY CAPTAIN.

"That's it!" says Danny. "Why don't we get him to vomit our flying saucer back up?"

"Yeah, right," I say. "That will get us a good mark. Ms. Livingstone will be really impressed by a pile of frothy dog vomit."

"No, I don't mean we'd hand it in," says Danny. "All we need are the aliens. We can build another flying saucer."

I can't believe it. Danny's actually had a good idea. It wouldn't be hard to build another flying saucer. And we still have the written part of the assignment.

"I guess it's worth a try," I say.

"But how do we get Sooty to be sick?" says Danny. "Is there a command for that?"

THINK VO5. WE ARE THE FIRST TO TREAD THESE PATHS.

"No," I say. "And if there was, Sooty wouldn't obey it anyway. We're going to have to *make* him sick."

"How?" says Danny. "Force-feed him dog food?"

"No," I say. "He can eat that forever and not be sick. Chocolate is what we need."

25

"Good idea," says Danny. "Chocolate always makes me think better."

"Not for us, you dope," I say. "For Sooty. One Easter, Sooty ate all my Easter eggs. A whole bag full. He was really sick then."

"But where are we going to get that much chocolate?" says Danny. "I don't have any money. Do you?"

"Relax," I say. "We don't need money. You stay here and guard Sooty. I'll be right back."

I go to the laundry room. Dad's secret chocolate supply is right at the back of the laundry room cupboard. I don't know why we call it his secret supply, really. The only thing secret about it is that he doesn't know that we all know it's there.

I push the bottles of disinfectant and cleaning stuff out of the way and pull out a plastic bag full of chocolate. There are three bags of chocolate-covered almonds, a bag of M&Ms, two family-sized bars of milk chocolate, half a dozen caramel Easter eggs, and a big tray of assorted chocolate truffles. If that doesn't make him sick, then nothing will.

I take the bag into the living room.

"Here, Sooty," I call. I unwrap a caramel nut swirl. I crunch the wrapper noisily in my hand.

26

That ought to do the trick. Sooty can never resist the sound of food being opened.

He pokes his head out from under the couch.

I wave the chocolate under his nose.

"Look, Sooty," I say. "Caramel nut swirl!"

Sooty wriggles the rest of his body out from under the couch, but he doesn't take the bait.

He just stands and looks at me. Maybe he's too full of flying saucer. Or maybe he remembers how much trouble he got into the time he ate all my Easter eggs.

I bite the caramel nut swirl in half.

"Mmmm," I say. "Yummy. Want a bit of this hand-picked peanut dipped in caramel and smothered in rich, dark chocolate, Sooty? It's delicious."

I don't know about Sooty, but it's working on Danny. He's practically drooling all over the carpet.

"Can I have one?" he says.

"Just one," I say. "Keep the rest for Sooty."

Danny picks one up and unwraps it.

I put mine under Sooty's nose.

"You know you want it," I say. "So have it! You deserve it."

Sooty sniffs it. He licks it and takes it into

27

his mouth and swallows it whole. He doesn't need any more encouragement. He starts wolfing down chocolates as fast as Danny and I can unwrap them. Every now and again, we have one as well. Well, to tell the truth, it's hard to tell who's eating more — Sooty or us. Danny has chocolate all around his mouth — it's dribbling down his chin onto his shirt.

Suddenly the door opens.

"Andy!" says Dad. "What do you think you're doing?"

I look up. Dad is home early.

"Dad!" I say. "I didn't expect you home this early!"

"Obviously not," he says. He bends down and picks up a chocolate wrapper. "Have you been eating my chocolates?"

"No, Dad . . ." I say. "It was Sooty! I came in here and they were everywhere."

I point at Sooty.

"Bad dog!" I say. "You're a very bad dog!"

Dad shakes his head. "Andy, do you really expect me to believe that?"

"Yes," I say.

"But it's all over your face," says Dad. "And Danny's, too."

Danny quickly pulls up his T-shirt and

28

wipes his face. But there's so much chocolate on his shirt that it only makes it worse.

"Um, yes," I say, "that's true. But we just wanted to make sure that the chocolate hadn't passed its expiration date . . . in case we had to take Sooty to the hospital."

"Yeah," says Danny. "Can't be too careful with expiration dates."

I think it's quite a good excuse, but Dad is not listening. He is beyond listening. He is getting ready to give a lecture.

"Andy," he says, "it's bad enough that you steal my chocolate."

"Yes, Dad."

When Dad is lecturing, I find it's best to just agree with everything he says. It seems to calm him down.

"And it's even worse that you compound your crime by eating my chocolate."

"Yes, Dad."

"But then to waste it on the dog — that is really stupid!"

"Yes, Dad."

"And then to *blame* the poor dog!"

"Yes, Dad."

"Do you really expect me to believe that he went into the laundry room, opened the cabi-

29

net door, pulled out the chocolates, carried them to the living room, and unwrapped them all by himself? What do you take me for — an idiot?"

"Yes, Dad."

"What?!"

Oops. Sometimes it's better not to agree.

"I mean, no, Dad."

Now he's *really* mad.

"Clean up this mess," he says. "And you can replace what you have eaten out of your own allowance."

"Yes, Dad."

He turns and leaves the room.

I look at Sooty.

"This is your fault," I say.

"Yeah," says Danny. "It's all your fault."

Sooty just sits down and scratches himself. He doesn't care.

"The least you could do is be sick!" I say.

He stares back at me.

"Come on, Sooty!" I say. "Be sick!"

"It's not working," says Danny.

Suddenly, I have a brainstorm. I'm not a smoker or anything, but I did have a puff once. I was with my cousin, David. He said I should learn to smoke because it really impresses girls.

But I didn't impress anybody. All I did was cough so much that I was sick. If I can get Sooty to smoke a cigarette, then maybe it will have the same effect on him.

"It doesn't matter," I say to Danny. "I've got a better idea. Let's make him smoke."

"Is he old enough?" says Danny.

"He is in dog years," I say. "Come on."

I grab Sooty by the collar, drag him outside, and lock him underneath the house.

"Wait there," I say. "We'll be back in a minute."

We go out into the street and search the sidewalk for butts. We find a couple and go back under the house. It's very cramped and dark, and we have to double over.

I find a box of matches and light one of the butts. I suck the smoke back.

It tastes horrible. I cough so hard I almost throw up. Perfect!

I offer the butt to Sooty, but he turns his head away. I try to put it in his mouth but he just keeps moving his head from side to side.

"Come on, Sooty," I wheeze. "Think how cool you'll look when you learn to smoke. And how tough. The girl dogs will all go for you for sure."

THIS IS A FIRE HYDRANT!!

TINY DOG.

IT DOES STUNT YOUR GROWTH!!

"Isn't this a little cruel?" says Danny. "I mean, won't it stunt his growth?"

"He's short already," I say. "He can hardly get any shorter."

"But what if he gets hooked?" says Danny.

"Then we'll call the Quit line," I say. "But first, we'll get back our aliens."

But Sooty has other ideas. He jerks his head away from me and knocks the butt out of my hands. It falls into my lap.

"Ahhhh!" I scream. I jump up.

WHACK!

My head hits the roof.

"Ouch!" I yell.

"Andy?" calls Mom. "Is that you under there?"

"No, Mom," I say, hoping that she will believe me and go away.

"Are you smoking?"

"No," I say.

"Then why can I smell smoke?" she says.

"It's Sooty," I say. "We're trying to get him to stop but he won't listen."

"Andy, get out here this minute!" says Mom.

We all crawl out.

Mom is standing there with her hands on her hips.

-POP-

POP

32

"That's the most pathetic excuse I've ever heard," she says. "When are you going to grow up and start taking responsibility for your actions?"

"But, Mom . . ." I say.

"No, listen to me," says Mom. "I know you think it looks cool and tough, and that it will make girls like you, but do you realize what smoking can do to your health?"

"But . . ." I say.

"It rots your lungs. It stunts your growth. It ruins your circulation. You'll get gangrene, and your toes will drop off. Is that what you want?"

"Are you getting all this, Sooty?" I say.

"I'm talking to you!" says Mom. "You two would be a lot better off playing outside in the fresh air than huddled under the house smoking. Why don't you go to the playground? The exercise would do you good."

The playground? How old does she think we are?

"But, Mom," I say, "playgrounds are for kids."

"Don't be silly," says Mom. "Playgrounds are for everybody."

"Why don't *you* go down there then?" I say.

"Well," says Mom, "because at my age,

33

swings and seesaws and merry-go-rounds make me feel ill, but if I were your age, I'd be down there in a flash."

I look at Danny.

Danny looks at me.

"That's it!" I say. "Great idea, Mom! Can we take Sooty?"

"Sure," says Mom, a little surprised by my sudden change of mind. "But no more smoking!"

"Okay," I say. "Did you hear that, Sooty? No more smoking!"

Mom rolls her eyes.

We grab Sooty and drag him down the driveway, across the street, and down to the playground.

"This should do the trick," I say to Danny. "Chocolate, smoking, and swinging — a lethal combination. Even for a dog with a cast-iron gut, like Sooty."

Sooty digs his claws into the sidewalk the whole way. Sometimes I swear he can understand English. I have to drag him by the collar while Danny pushes him along from behind.

Finally, we make it to the playground.

"Gee," says Danny. "This place has changed."

He's right. The playground is not what it

34

used to be. They've removed all the old metal stuff we used to play on and replaced it with a load of brightly colored plastic junk. It's strictly for babies. There are still swings, but they're not the big ones — just the ones that look like rubber underpants with little safety chains across the front. Still, they'll be perfect for Sooty.

He's not too keen on the idea, though. He's straining to get away.

"Don't worry, Sooty," I say. "We're not mad at you. We're just going to have some fun."

I try to pick him up, but he's twisting and turning and I can't get a good grip.

"Give me a hand, Danny," I say.

But Danny is not beside me. I look up. He's climbing across the top of a yellow dome.

"Hey!" he calls. "Your mom was right. This is pretty good! We should come here more often."

"Danny!" I yell. "Get over here right now! Don't you realize what's at stake?"

"Just one more time?" he says.

"Danny!"

Danny jumps off the dome and comes running over.

I put my hands around Sooty's chest and hold him just above the swing. As I lower him

FUN WITH RUBBER UNDERPANTS.

STRETCH THEM.

INFLATE THEM WITH GAS.

FLOAT AWAY ON THEM

into the rubber seat, Danny puts Sooty's hind legs through the legholes. I pull the chain across and lock it into position.

I run around behind the swing, pull it back, and push it as hard as I can.

Sooty goes swinging up into the air. He barks crazily. The swing comes whooshing back and I push it even harder. He barks even louder.

"Hey!" says a voice behind us. "Take that dog out of there!"

I turn around.

It's my neighbor, Mr. Broadbent. He doesn't like me very much. I think it's got something to do with the time I accidentally set his fence on fire.

"Let him go!" he says.

"But Sooty likes it," I say. "He just loves the swing."

"Then why is he barking like that?" says Mr. Broadbent.

"He's barking for joy," I say, giving the swing another push. All I've got to do is keep Mr. Broadbent talking. A couple more swings should do it. Just a couple more.

"If you don't let that dog out of there, I'm going to call the ASPCA," says Mr. Broadbent.

"Actually, it's the ASPCA who told me to do this," I say. "They said swinging is good for dogs. It makes them mentally happy. You should try it."

"I don't have a dog," he says.

"I meant for you," I say.

I push Sooty again.

"Are you going to stop that or do I have to come over there and make you?" says Mr. Broadbent.

"Just one more and I'm through," I say.

I give Sooty one last big push.

Sooty flies up, up, up into the air.

But he doesn't come back down again.

He keeps going.

He flies out of the swing like he's been shot out of a cannon. He travels across the park and lands out of sight behind some trees.

Mr. Broadbent shakes his head.

"That poor dog," he says.

"How could I know that was going to happen?" I say. "This playground equipment is dangerous. The seat belts are hopeless!"

I grab Danny.

"Come on," I say. "We have to catch him. He could puke at any moment!"

We run toward the trees.

WHEN AN OLD VACUUM DIES, ITS MATE WILL STAY WITH THE BODY FOR MONTHS, HOWLING AT THE MOON.

FOR MORE ON VACUUM BEHAVIOR, TURN TO PG.128.

We find Sooty walking around and around the base of a large pine tree.

"There he is!" says Danny. "Looks like he's going to be sick."

"Shush," I say. "I don't want him to know we're here. He might run off."

We hide behind a park bench and watch him.

Sooty circles the tree.

Then he stops.

Maybe the combination of chocolate, smoke, swinging, and flying through the air has done the trick. He's finally going to be sick.

But Sooty doesn't throw up. He lifts his leg and wees on the tree trunk.

Danny giggles.

"Having fun, boys?" says a voice behind us.

I turn around.

Oh no.

I'm staring at a big slobbering rottweiler.

I look up.

It's Roseanne O'Reilly . . . and Lisa Mackney. They must be taking Roseanne's rottweiler for a walk.

Roseanne turns to Lisa.

"Spying on a dog having a wee is kind of pathetic, don't you think?" she says.

38

"No," says Lisa. "It's not kind of pathetic. It's definitely pathetic."

"No, you don't understand," I say. "I can explain. . . ."

"Yeah," says Danny. "We didn't want to watch him having a wee. We were hoping he was going to be sick."

Lisa and Roseanne look horrified.

"That's even worse," says Roseanne. "Come on, Lisa. Let's get away from these psychos."

They walk off. Lisa looks sadly back at me over her shoulder.

Damn. Of all the parks she could have come into, why did she have to come into this one? And why right now? I want to run after her and explain, but I can't leave Sooty. Stupid dog. This is all his fault.

Roseanne calls to her rottweiler.

He's over at the tree sniffing at the place where Sooty just lifted his leg.

Uh-oh.

They start growling and circling each other. The hairs rise into spiky patterns on their backs.

The rottweiler lunges at Sooty and sinks his teeth into Sooty's throat.

"No, Slayer!" screams Roseanne.

I jump up and run toward them.

I grab Sooty by the tail and pull him up into the air. But Slayer comes too, still attached to Sooty's neck.

For a moment I'm holding both dogs in the air, but then Slayer loses his grip and falls to the ground. He jumps back up and snaps at Sooty.

I swing Sooty away from him, but he follows, lunging and snapping. I have to keep swinging Sooty around and around and around.

"Do something, Roseanne!" screams Lisa.

"No, Slayer," calls Roseanne again. "Bad dog!"

"Go, Andy!" yells Danny.

"Do something, Danny!" I scream.

Danny picks up a pinecone and throws it at Slayer.

It hits me in the head. Ouch! Right where I bumped it earlier under the house.

"Sorry!" says Danny.

He tries again. This one is a better shot. It hits Slayer in the side.

Slayer stops trying to bite Sooty and starts trying to bite me instead.

He sinks his teeth into my leg.

"*Aaggh!*" I yell.

I drop Sooty.

Sooty sprints away toward home.

"Quick, Danny!" I yell.

I try to run after Sooty, but I'm dizzy from spinning around, and I run into a tree.

Ouch.

Danny helps me up.

Lisa and Roseanne are just standing there shaking their heads and laughing.

I want to tell Roseanne off for not keeping her crazy dog on a leash, but I don't have time for that now. We have to catch Sooty.

Danny and I take off after him. We chase him all the way home.

When we get there, Sooty is in the backyard, lying on the grass, panting.

Danny and I flop down beside him.

"Poor dog," says Danny. "Look at him. He's exhausted."

Poor dog? What about me? I've been yelled at by Dad, lost at least ten weeks' allowance, whacked my head, been yelled at by Mom, been humiliated in front of Lisa, hit by a pinecone, bitten by a dog, and had a head-on collision with a tree. And Sooty still hasn't been sick. It's not fair.

41

"What now?" says Danny.

"I hate to say it," I say, "but I think we're going to have to tell Ms. Livingstone the truth."

"But you said . . ." says Danny. "You said . . ."

"I know, Danny," I say. "But that was before we'd tried everything. He's not going to throw up. The only thing left is to wait until it comes out the other end, and there's no way I'm going to touch that."

"Hang on," says Danny, grabbing my arm so hard it hurts. "Look!"

He's pointing toward Sooty.

I don't believe it.

Sooty's wandered to the edge of the lawn and is being sick.

It's the most wonderful thing I've ever seen!

"Good dog, Sooty," I say. "Bring it all up. You'll feel better."

He coughs a few more times and walks away.

"Come on, Danny," I say. "We've got work to do."

We go over and kneel beside the pile of steaming, frothy goo. It's a yellowy sort of color, with patches of brown.

I grab a stick and start poking at it, looking for the flying saucer.

CLOSE-UP ON DOG VOMIT.

PIECE OF DUG-UP, RECENTLY DEAD, PET RABBIT.

CAT FUR

PIECES OF BROCCOLI FED TO IT FROM LAST NIGHT'S DINNER

PIECE OF PAPER BOY'S LEG

42

OF COURSE ALL MY MECHANICAL BIRD FRIENDS THINK...

Danny does the same.

I find a piece of what I think is our assignment, but on closer examination it turns out to be part of a chocolate wrapper.

Searching through Sooty's vomit with a stick is not exactly my idea of great afternoon entertainment. But what's really bad is that there's no trace of the flying saucer. Or the aliens.

I push aside another lump of half-chewed chocolate, and then I see something green. There they are! Our aliens!

"Danny!" I say. "I found them!"

Danny stares down into Sooty's sick and smiles widely.

"I bet those guys are pleased to see us," he says.

"*EEERRRGGHHH!* I don't believe you two!" says a voice behind us.

I turn around. It's Jen.

"You are gross!" she says. "I've never heard of anyone weird enough to play with their own vomit!"

"It's not my vomit," I say. "It's Sooty's!"

"I'm going to tell Mom," she says, putting her hand up to her mouth. "You two need help. Serious professional help!"

THINGS TO BE FOUND IN A NORMAL PILE OF DOG VOMIT.

FLUFFY'S COLLAR.

DING!

FLUFFY'S BELL.

WHY ME?

STING

THE QUEEN'S MOTHER

FLUFFY

43

THAT THE PICTURES ARE THE BEST BIT.

HOW TO
MAKE YOUR
DOG SICK.

MAKE IT
SLEEP IN
YOUR
UNDERPANTS
DRAWER.

BLEAGH!

PUT YOUR
SOCKS OVER
ITS NOSE.

TELL IT
YOUR LIFE
STORY.

Jen turns and starts to run.

I'm already in enough trouble. I don't really think Mom needs to know about this.

"Quick, Danny," I say. "Help me stop her!"

We get up and run after her. I grab Jen's shoulder.

"Get your pukey hands off me!" she screams. She shakes us off and runs up the steps and into the house.

"That's all I need," I say, turning back to Danny. "But at least we found the aliens."

"Oh no," says Danny, "look!"

Sooty has returned to his vomit. And he's eating it like he hasn't eaten for a week.

"Get away from that, you crazy dog!" I scream.

We run over to scare him away, but it's too late. They're gone. He's eaten them.

Again.

"You stupid dog!" I yell. "You ate our aliens! Twice! I'm going to kill you!"

I put my hands around his throat and start to squeeze.

"Andy!" says Mom sharply. "What is wrong with you today?"

She's standing outside the back door.

I let Sooty go.

44

THE STORIES
ARE OK.
BUT THE
DRAWINGS
ARE SOOO
FUNNY.

"Nothing, Mom," I say.

"Nothing?" she says. "Your father told me about the chocolate. And Mr. Broadbent has just been on the phone telling me what you were doing to Sooty in the playground. Then Jen comes in and says you vomited and she saw you playing with it. And now I find you strangling the poor dog."

"But . . ." I say.

"No more of your pathetic excuses," she says. "Please! Until you learn to treat Sooty better, you can sleep in his kennel and he can have your bed."

She turns and storms back inside.

I look at Sooty. This is all his fault.

I kneel down, hold his head, and stare into his eyes.

"Are you happy now?" I say.

He wags his tail, leans forward, and licks my mouth.

I think I'm going to be sick.

BUT THAT'S MECHANICAL BIRDS FOR YOU. JUST A FUNNY, FUNNY GROUP.

45

DID I TELL YOU ABOUT OUR LAST MECHO-BIRD CAMP? WOW!

A Crazy, BAD, Dumb, Bad, Bad, Dumb, CRAZY, BAD IDEA

SCHOOL CARNIVAL.

LUCKY DIP.

SPIT!

I'm standing in the middle of the school ball field.

I'm trembling.

And I'm covered in sweat.

Am I crazy to be doing this?

No.

In fact, I'd be crazy *not* to do it.

This sort of opportunity doesn't present itself every day. Besides, it's a perfect morning for flying. The sky is clear, and it's not too windy.

Mr. Pickett, Danny's dad, is running this year's school carnival. It's today. Danny and I have been here since 6 A.M. helping him set up. For the last hour, we've been filling balloons with helium. We're going to put them along the school fence and front gates. We've also got some weather balloons that were donated by the local army surplus store. We've painted a letter on each one. Put them together and they spell "CARNIVAL." Mr. Pickett's idea is to attach them to eight really long pieces of rope and float them high above the school to let people know the carnival is today. Which is what's going to happen. Eventually. But first I'm just going to take them for a little joy flight.

Danny and I have tied two enormous bunches of party balloons to the front straps of my backpack, and the eight giant weather balloons to the back of it.

The balloons are tugging at my backpack, pulling me upward. My toes are just touching the ground. The only thing keeping me from floating off is that Danny is holding tightly to my arm and the rope around my waist.

"Okay," I say to Danny. "Let the rope out about thirty feet and then haul me back in. Got that?"

"Are you really sure you want to do this?" he says. "I don't think it's a good idea."

"Are you kidding?" I say. "Of course it's a good idea! It's a great idea! It's a brilliant idea! It's perfectly safe. Just don't let go of the rope."

MR. SCRIBBLE MEETS Mr. ERASER.

BARGH!

IS THIS THE END FOR Mr. SCRIBBLE?

47

NOTICE: THE MECHANICAL BIRD HAS BEEN REPLACED BY A SIMPLE BOX...BY ORDER OF THE AUTHOR

Danny shakes his head.

"I won't let go," he says. "You can count on me."

I'm not leaving anything to chance, though. That's why I'm holding a long sharp stick. Just in case.

If Danny does let go, then all I'll have to do is burst a couple of balloons and I'll descend slowly and safely. It can't go wrong.

"Come on, Danny," I say. "Before your dad gets back. He said he'd only be gone for half an hour. We don't have much time."

"Are you ready?" says Danny.

"Roger," I say.

"Roger?" says Danny, looking around. "Who's Roger?"

"Nobody," I sigh. "It's what pilots say. It means yes."

"Oh yeah," says Danny. "I forgot. I'm just a little nervous. If Dad finds out about this, he's going to kill us."

"Come on, Dan," I say. "Your dad will never know. I'm just going straight up and straight down."

Danny nods.

"All right, Roger," he says. "Have fun."

He lets go of my arm.

48

My backpack pulls even harder against my chest, and I quickly start floating upward.

I can't believe it. It's working. I've always wanted to fly, and now I am.

I flap my arms and call down to Danny.

"Look at me!" I say. "I'm flying!"

"Go, Roger!" yells Danny.

"Stop calling me Roger, you idiot!" I yell.

"Roger, Roger!" yells Danny.

I shake my head. I can't believe I'm trusting this moron with my life.

I look all around me. It's a great view. I can see forever. The neighborhood is laid out below me like a little toy village. And there's my house! Wow!

I wish I could stay up here all day, but it's cold, and the wind is much stronger this far up. I should have worn a sweater.

"Danny!" I yell. "That's enough. Bring me down!"

He looks pretty small from up here, like a little boy flying a kite.

He waves back. Then he starts letting out the rope to make me go higher. He obviously can't hear me.

"No, Danny!" I scream. "Not higher! Lower!"

THAT'S MUCH BETTER

CATE AND ANNA'S BIRTHDAY CAKE.

I point toward the ground.

He points at me and points back to the ground and shrugs.

I nod wildly.

"Yes, Danny!" I yell. "Down!"

He starts trying to pull me in, but he seems to be having trouble. The wind is really strong up here, and I'm starting to drift toward the edge of the ball field.

Danny is leaning back, straining on the rope. But it's no use. He's not pulling me down — I'm pulling him along.

Uh-oh.

This is not fun anymore. And the wind seems to be getting even stronger.

"Come on, Danny!" I call. "You can do it!"

But he can't hear me. And he can't do it, either. He is being dragged to the edge of the ball field where it slopes steeply away to the fence. He takes two giant steps, trips, and tumbles down the hill. . . .

I feel myself whoosh high and fast into the air. Danny has let go of the rope!

I can see him lying at the bottom of the bank, holding his leg. He's getting smaller and smaller and smaller.

Aaaaggghhh! I'm floating away!

50

A BOX

What am I going to do?

How am I going to get down?

What if I just keep going up and up and up until I end up out in space?

This was a bad idea.

A dumb idea.

A crazy idea.

A bad, dumb, crazy idea.

A crazy, bad, dumb, bad, bad, dumb, crazy, bad idea.

And I've only got myself to blame. Which makes it even worse. I hate that.

Hang on. The stick! I forgot about my stick!

I don't have to worry about a thing. All I have to do is burst a couple of balloons and I'll go down instead of up. Mr. Pickett won't be happy about me bursting the balloons, but at least I won't just disappear and never be seen again, which will make *me* happy.

I raise the stick as high above my head as I can. I try to poke a hole in the "C" balloon, but it just bobs away. The skin is tougher than I thought. I jab at the "R" balloon. It bobs away as well. I try some of the party balloons, but it's no use. There's nothing to push against. This stick was another bad, dumb, crazy idea.

I poke a few more times, but my neck's get-

FLOATING AWAY...

A PAGE NUMBER BOX.

ting really sore from looking up at the balloons. I give up and turn around.

Oh no.

In front of me is the scariest thing I've ever seen.

High-voltage power lines.

There must be at least fifty of them — stretching in front of me like a gigantic horizontal spiderweb.

And I'm heading straight toward them.

If I don't do something fast, I'm going to hit the lines and fry like a mosquito in a bug zapper.

I have to get rid of some of these balloons.

I can't pop them, but maybe I can untie them.

I pull at the knots tying the party balloons to my backpack, but I can't get them undone. They're too tight. It'll take me ages to get them untied. Time I don't have.

Maybe I should just take the backpack off and let myself fall to the ground. But that would kill me. But so will the wires.

What to do? Fry or splatter? Splatter or fry?

Actually, I'd rather die of old age.

My only hope of that, though, is to go *over* the power lines. But how? How do I get myself up higher?

BOX: A RIGID CONTAINER HAVING 4 SIDES, A BOTTOM AND A TOP.

52

I know! I could toss some stuff. The more I can get rid of, the higher I'll go.

I'll start with this stupid stick. It was no help at all.

I drop it. It falls through the air like a spear. Lucky there's nothing but grass and trees underneath me.

What else can I get rid of?

I look at my sneakers. The soles alone must weigh at least two pounds. They're brand-new, but they're going to have to go.

I raise my feet up, untie the laces, and pull off the sneakers. My socks as well. They go sailing downward.

But I'm still not high enough. I need to get rid of more.

I untie the rope from around my waist and let it go. I search through the pockets of my jeans and pull out everything I've got. A used Band-Aid. A half-eaten candy bar. A chewing-gum wrapper. A dead cockroach — at least I think it's dead. My wallet. It's got ten dollars in it. I saved it to spend at the carnival. But I have to let it go. It kills me to drop all this stuff, but it will really kill me to keep it.

I rummage deep in my shirt pockets. I pull out a photograph of Lisa Mackney. No, not

53

OTHER PICTURES OF LISA.

that. Anything but that. I cut it out of our school newspaper. It's not a very good picture, because it only catches her profile. Well, more like the back of her head — most of which is covered by the back of somebody else's head — but I know it's her. And it's all I have. I can't throw it away.

I look at the power lines.

I've made a lot of progress. A lot of very good progress. I'm a little bit higher than I was. But still not high enough. I need to lose something else. But I haven't got anything else. Except my pants, that is.

I watch as my jeans drop away toward the ground.

I hate to see them go. They're my favorite pair. And it's freezing up here. If I don't fry on the wires, I'll probably die of exposure.

The wires are getting closer, but unless I get a little higher, I'm not going to clear them.

I look at Lisa's photograph in my hand. I'm going to have to let her go.

It flutters and spirals away. It's the saddest thing I've ever seen in my life.

But also the most fantastic.

Because it's saved my life.

Lisa Mackney has saved my life!

54 BOTTOM

I lift my legs, curl my toes, and clear the power lines with less than an inch to spare. I hear the deadly hum of the electricity as I skim over the top. If this hadn't been such a crazy, bad, dumb, bad, bad, dumb, crazy, bad idea in the first place, I would be very proud of myself.

I take a few deep breaths and try to relax. But not for long. Because now I've got a new problem. Well, an old problem actually but it's getting worse. I've got goose bumps all over my legs and my toes are turning purple. And I'm still no closer to the ground. How am I going to get down and get back to the school before Mr. Pickett does?

I'm going to have to try to untie the party balloons again.

I've got human bumps all over my legs.

YOU GOOSE!

I work away at the knots. It's hard because not only are they tied on very tightly, but my fingers are almost numb with cold.

Finally, I loosen the knots and untie the balloons from the shoulder strap of my backpack. There must be at least two hundred of them. They fly into the sky above me like I just won a million bucks on a game show.

I begin to drop quickly. They were giving me more lift than I realized. For a moment, I'm worried that I'm going to keep dropping and

A DIFFERENT BOTTOM.

1. MEOW LIKE A CAT TO GET NEXT-DOOR'S DOG BARKING.

2. BANG TWO METAL TRASH CAN LIDS. TOGETHER TO GET THE DOG ON THE OTHER SIDE HOWLING.

3. ROLL A METAL TRASH CAN LID DOWN THE SIDEWALK.

4. MAKE SURE THE DOGS ARE ALL BARKING.

5. CALL THE POLICE AND ASK THEM TO COME OVER... HOPE THEY USE THE SIREN.

not stop, but I level out just a little above the treetops. That's better. Not perfect, but a lot better. It beats hovering above high-altitude high-voltage lines any day.

I'm floating slowly over the roofs of houses. I can see into all the backyards. A dog is going nuts. Barking and jumping up at me. It sets off other dogs, and soon there's a chorus of barking and howling.

Some kids are pointing and waving at me. I wave back. They run out of their yard and onto the street and begin following me. They are joined by others, and within minutes there's a small crowd of people following me. Not just kids, either. There are a few adults, as well. One of them is pointing a video camera at me. Probably hoping I'll have an accident so he can send it to one of those funniest-home-video shows.

"Don't just watch me!" I yell. "Help me!"

"What do you want us to do?" yells a woman.

Now that's a very good question.

I don't exactly know.

They don't teach you how to deal with situations like this in school. That's the trouble with school. They don't teach you anything useful. There should be a subject called "What to do if you find yourself floating about sixty feet

56 BOX.

off the ground with no pants on and eight large weather balloons attached to your backpack." Or, even better, they could deal with this and many other situations by lumping them together under one subject called "Crazy, bad, dumb, bad, bad, dumb, crazy, bad ideas." Now *that* would be useful.

I'm heading toward a long row of pine trees. I can hear buzzing and whining. Oh no, not more power lines! No, it's louder than that.

A BUSY DAY AT THE MODEL CHICKEN LEG CLUB.

As I float over the tops of the pine trees, I see lots of people. They are all looking up, as if they've been waiting for me to appear. But it's not me they're looking at.

Gulp.

The air is filled with model airplanes. They are looping and diving around one another.

MAKE FUN OF CHICKEN LEGS WILL YOU!

I suddenly realize what this is.

It's the local model airplane club. They're putting on a display at the school carnival today. They must be practicing.

People are pointing and laughing at me.

"Look out!" I yell. "I'm coming through!"

But there's too much noise. And the men flying the planes are too busy turning the knobs on their remote control units to even notice me.

57

CHICKEN LEG

A CLOSE
SHAVE AT
THE MODEL
PLANE
CLUB.

I float right into the middle of the action. The planes are swooping and diving and whining around me like a pack of killer mosquitoes. But I can't swat them. They're much too big for that, and their propellers look much too sharp.

I hear a particularly loud whine behind me.

I turn my head and see a large biplane with orange wings.

Uh-oh. I'm in trouble.

Or am I?

This could be just what I need to get me away from here and back to the school. I might even beat Danny's dad.

I watch as the plane flies closer and closer. I flex my fingers and wait for my chance. I'm only going to get one shot at this.

I KNOW
WHO YOU
ARE AND
WHERE
YOU LIVE...

ONE WHO
LAUGHS AT
CHICKEN
LEGS.

As it passes me, I shoot my hand out and grab on to its tail.

It starts pulling me away at high speed. I can feel the wind from the propeller on my face.

I carefully turn the plane toward the right. I fly around in a wide semicircle and head back toward the school.

I hear yelling.

"Hey, you little thief! Let go of my plane!" calls a man in a red cap.

WHEEL

"I'm not stealing it," I yell. "I'm just borrowing it. I'll bring it back. I promise!"

But he obviously doesn't believe me. He is furiously working away at his controls and I feel the plane start to turn back again.

"Oh, no you don't," I say. I reach over and pull the aerial out of the cockpit of the plane. I'm in control now.

I turn the plane toward the school and travel back the way I came. Over the houses, over the yard. It's the same as before except now I'm traveling ten times faster, and this time I go *under* the power lines instead of over them.

I can see the school ball field ahead of me. There are a few more people there now than when I left. They're unpacking cars and setting up tables. The jumping castle is being inflated. Imagine one of them filled with helium. Now that is a good idea. You could float *really* high.

There's Danny at the edge of the ball field. He's still sitting on the ground, holding his leg. He's looking up, talking to somebody. Who is that?

Oh no.

It's Mr. Pickett!

Rats. I didn't beat him. I'm going to get in trouble after all.

59

HORSE HEAD.

They look up and see me.

Danny gets to his feet and waves.

I point the plane downward and head toward the baseball diamond. It will make a great landing strip.

When I'm a few yards from the field, I straighten the plane up and level out.

"Grab me!" I yell.

Mr. Pickett starts running. He wraps his arms around my legs and pulls me to the ground.

Danny limps over and takes the plane out of my hand. He flicks the throttle switch off.

"That was so cool!" he says. "You're amazing!"

"Shut up!" growls Mr. Pickett. He keeps hold of me while he takes the pack off my back. "What on earth did you think you were doing?" he yells. "Of all the irresponsible, foolhardy stunts to pull!"

"It's not his fault, Dad," says Danny. "I shouldn't have let go of the rope."

"That's beside the point!" yells Mr. Pickett. "He should never have been up there in the first place!"

Danny looks at me and shrugs. It was a

60

good try and I appreciate it, but Mr. Pickett is on a roll.

"You could have been killed!" he says and points at the sky. "These balloons were supposed to be used to advertise the carnival. They should have been up there by now. Instead, I come back and find that you've taken them for a joy flight. An insanely dangerous one, I might add!"

I look over Mr. Pickett's shoulder.

The small crowd that was following me through the streets is coming through the gates of the school. But it's not a small crowd anymore. It's huge!

There are kids, adults, dogs, cars, police, an angry-looking man in a red cap, and even a television news van with a satellite dish on the roof. A cameraman is hanging out the window with his camera pointed at us. They must be transmitting live footage back to their newsroom.

Wow! I'm going to be on TV. I'm famous. That's great, but I wish I had some pants on.

Mr. Pickett pauses. He's so mad he can't think of what to say next.

A little kid comes up behind him and tugs on his sweater.

WE'VE GOT YOU.

61

He wheels around and looks down.

"What do you want?" he growls.

"How much for a ride on the balloons?" says the kid, pointing to my pack, which Mr. Pickett is still holding.

"What?" he says.

He looks up and notices the crowd. There are people everywhere. Already there's a long line at the hot-dog stand and the drinks booth. Chasing me through the streets has obviously made everyone pretty hungry and thirsty.

Business is booming. Mr. Pickett can't be mad at me now. I wish I could say the same for the man in the red cap, though. He snatches his plane from Danny and walks up to me.

"I want a word with you," he says.

"Smile!" calls a newspaper photographer.

The man turns. He smiles for the camera. Mr. Pickett puts his arm around my shoulder and smiles, too.

"Remind me to murder you later," he grunts.

I grin.

Looking at the crowd I've gathered, I can't help thinking that my balloon flight wasn't such a bad idea after all.

62

In fact, it was a good idea.

A great idea.

A brilliant idea.

A good, great, brilliant, great, great, brilliant, good, great idea.

63

TRASH

It's Tuesday night.

A very important night.

And not just because it's Valentine's Day, either.

It's trash night.

And what's so important about trash night?

Well, according to my mom and dad, the health of the entire neighborhood depends on me remembering to put the trash out.

Because if I forget to put the can out, the garbage men can't empty the can.

And if the garbage men can't empty the can, then we can't fit any more trash into it.

And if we can't fit any more trash into the can, then the trash will spill out over the top and onto the ground.

And if there's trash on the ground, then the rats will come, and if the rats come, people will get sick, disease and pestilence will spread throughout the neighborhood, and everyone will die.

And the worst thing is that I will get the blame.

That's why trash night is the most important night of the week: The fate of the neighborhood is in my hands. Every man, woman, and child is counting on me to remember to put the trash out.

And I haven't failed them yet.

I never forget.

Each week I tie a piece of white string around the little finger on my left hand to remind me.

The trouble is, tonight I've tied it a bit too tight and it's making my little finger throb. It's so tight that I can't get the knot undone. I'm going to have to cut it with a pair of scissors.

I go downstairs to the kitchen.

I pass Dad in the living room.

"Have you remembered what night this is?" he says.

"Yes, Dad," I say.

"Have you put the trash out yet?"

THESE
ARE A
FEW OF
ROVER'S
FAVORITE
THINGS.

1.

KNOCKING
OVER TRASH
CANS.

2.

HELPING
OTHER
DOGS
KNOCK
OVER TRASH
CANS

3.

CHASING
CATS INTO
TRASH CANS
AND TAPING
THEM UP.

4.

KNOCKING
OVER
MORE TRASH
CANS.

I AGREE.

"Not yet," I say.

"Well, don't forget," he says, "I don't want garbage spilling out all over the ground. It will attract rats and . . ."

"I know, Dad." I sigh. "If the rats come, people will get sick, disease and pestilence will spread throughout the neighborhood, and everyone will die."

"You think it's all a big joke, don't you?" he says, leaning forward in his chair and pointing his finger at me. "Well, we'll see how much of a joke it is when we're up to our ankles in trash and rats and you've got bubonic plague and you've got boils all over your body, funny-boy! And we'll all have a good laugh when pieces of your lungs come flying out of your mouth and . . ."

"Okay, Dad!" I say, "I get the picture! I'm going to put the can out, all right?"

"Now?" he says.

"In a minute," I say. "Right after I cut this string off my finger."

"Don't forget," he says.

"I won't, Dad," I say. "I promise."

I swear my dad's getting crazier by the day. I go into the kitchen, pull open the second drawer, and start rummaging around for the scissors.

Mom comes into the room.

"Have you put the trash out?" she says.

"Not yet, Mom," I say. "I'm just about to."

"Well, don't forget," she says. "We don't want . . ."

"Rats," I say.

"How did you know I was going to say that?" she says.

"A lucky guess," I say.

The phone rings.

I go to pick it up.

REASONS WHY YOU SHOULD NOT RUMMAGE IN DRAWERS THAT CONTAIN SCISSORS.

"Don't touch that!" says Jen, pushing past me and beating me to the phone. "That'll be Craig. Besides, shouldn't you be putting the trash out? It stinks — I can smell it from my room."

"I'm surprised you can smell anything above your own stink," I say. Jen makes a face and picks up the phone.

I just keep standing there. She hates it when I listen in on her calls.

Jen puts her hand over the mouthpiece.

"Mom," she says, "Andy's listening to my call."

67

WHAT?

"I am not!" I say. "How can I be listening if you haven't even started talking?"

"You're *going* to listen," she says.

"Pardon?" I say.

"I said 'you're *going* to listen,'" says Jen in a louder voice.

"What?" I say. "I can't hear you. I think I've gone deaf."

"Mom!" says Jen.

"Andy." Mom sighs. "You've got a job to do. Just go and do it."

"All right," I say, but I don't move. I just keep standing near the phone.

"Andy," says Jen.

"Okay, okay!" I say. "I'm going."

"That's not what I'm talking about," she says, holding the receiver toward me. "It's for you."

"For me?" I say.

"Yes," says Jen. "Hard to believe, isn't it, but apparently someone wants to talk to you."

"Who?" I say. "Who is it?"

"Whom shall I say is calling?" Jen says into the phone.

She smirks.

"It's Lisa Mackney," she says.

"Lisa Mackney?" I say. "Are you sure?"

68

"Do you want me to ask her if she's sure she's Lisa Mackney?" she says.

"No!" I say, grabbing the receiver.

Lisa Mackney! Wow! She must have got my Valentine's card. I slipped it into her bag this morning. I wonder how she guessed it was from me. Maybe the perfume on the envelope gave me away. Well, it wasn't exactly perfume. I couldn't find any, so I sprayed it with the pine-scented air freshener we use in the bathroom. It went all over my clothes, and I stunk of it all day. I guess she must have noticed.

Jen is still standing beside the phone.

"Mom!" I say. "Jen's listening to my call!"

"As if I'd want to listen to one of your juvenile phone calls," she says, walking out of the room. "I've *got* a life."

"Hello?" I say.

"Hi, Andy — it's Lisa," she says.

"Oh, um, er . . ." I stutter, trying to think of something clever to say. "Hi!"

"I hope you don't mind me calling you," she says.

Is she kidding? It's only the best thing that has ever happened in the history of the world. But I can't say this. She might think I'm making fun of her. I have to act cool.

69

HOW TO
CONVINCE
YOUR FRIENDS
YOU ARE NOT
A LOSER.

DYE YOUR
HAIR
GREEN.

BUY AN
INFLATABLE
MUSCLE
SHIRT.

PAY GIRLS TO
HANG AROUND
YOU.

GET YOUR MOM
TO CALL UP
EVERYONE
AND TELL
THEM.

"No," I say.

I can't think of anything else to say, which is funny because I've got so much to say. I want to tell her how beautiful she is and how much I love her and how I wish she would be my girl-friend . . . but I can't find the words.

"You're not busy, are you?" she says. "I can call back later if you'd like."

What do I say to this?

If I say I'm not busy, she might think I'm some sort of loser with nothing better to do than just sit around the house. But if I say I am busy putting the trash out, she might think that I'm some sort of loser with nothing better to do than put the trash out.

I know honesty is supposed to be the best policy, but in this case, I think that dishonesty is even better.

"No, I'm just taking a breather," I say. "I've been doing some weight training . . . those five-hundred-pound weights can be pretty tough."

"You do weight training?" she says.

"Oh, a little," I say.

"A little?" she says. "Five hundred pounds is a lot!"

"Oh not really," I say. "That's just a warm-

70

up. It's the thousand-pound weights that are really hard."

I hear Lisa gasp.

So far, so good. I think she's suitably impressed.

"Andy," she says, "can you be serious for a moment?"

"Huh?" I say. "I was being serious!"

Dishonest, but serious.

"I need to talk to you," she says. "It's important. I need to ask you a question. A serious question."

"Okay," I say. "What is it?"

"Did you send me the card?"

"What card?" I say, playing dumb.

"The Valentine's card," she says.

"Oh, that card," I say, as casually as I can. "Yes, I did."

"I thought so!" she says.

There's an uncomfortable silence. I'm not sure what to say next.

"I wanted to thank you," she says.

"That's okay," I say.

"No, I meant in person," she says. "I was wondering if we could meet tomorrow morning? Before school?"

THE NIGHT OF THE CHICKEN-LEGS FROM AUSTROLAUP-14.

I can't believe it! She's practically asking me out on a date!

"Andy?" she says. "Are you there?"

No, I'm not here. I'm somewhere between Earth and the moon I'm so happy. I have to try to come back. I have to answer her.

"Yes!" I say. "I'm here. Where would you like to meet?"

"How about outside the park near the school?" she says. "About 8:30?"

"Okay, Lisa," I say. I want to get off the phone now before I say anything stupid. "See you then."

"See you," she says. "And, Andy?"

"Yes?" I say.

"It wasn't a joke, was it?"

"What?" I say.

"The card?"

"No!" I say.

"Good," she says. "I'm really looking forward to it."

"Me, too," I say. I want to add, "Because you're beautiful and I love you," but I can't actually make the words because my mouth is just opening and closing like a fish.

I hang up.

I can't believe it.

72

The most beautiful girl in the world just called me and asked me out on a date. What if she asks me to go out with her? Can she do that? Can a girl ask a boy? I don't see why not. What if she asks me to marry her? Can we do that? Are we old enough? Will I need a ring? Or does the one who asks have to give the ring? What if she asks me to kiss her? I've never kissed a girl before. Not really. Not on the lips. How do you do that? I'd better go and practice on my mirror.

THE KISS.

I don't walk back up the stairs. I float.

Lisa called me.

Lisa called me and asked me out.

She asked me out.

I have to keep repeating it so that I can believe it.

Lisa called me.

She asked me out.

I didn't call her. She called me. She must really like me after all. After everything bad that's happened.

I float into my room and flop onto my bed.

She loves me.

She loves me.

I lie on my bed and think about tomorrow morning.

73

I can see it now.

I'm walking up the road to the park. I have a dozen roses in my arms.

Lisa is standing there, looking beautiful.

Everything around her is sort of blurry, like in one of those romantic photos they have in the front of photo shops, but she is in the middle in perfect focus.

She smiles and waves.

"Hi, Lisa," I say, in a deep, strong, and confident voice.

She looks into my eyes.

I look into hers. I feel like I'm melting.

"Hi," she says in a voice so soft and beautiful that she sounds like an angel.

I give her the roses.

"These are for you," I say.

HER EYES
FILL WITH
TEARS

FROM PG. 129
FURTHER
DETAILS
OF DR.
WOMKLE'S
DREAM
DE-NEBULIZER
HAVE BEEN
MOVED TO
PAGE: 90

She looks at the roses. Her eyes fill with tears.

"They're beautiful," she sobs. "Just beautiful . . ."

"Not as beautiful as you," I say, putting my arms around her.

I bury my face in her soft, perfumed hair — every strand shining like it's spun from the finest gossamer.

YUM!
SPLUNCH.
CHOMP.

"Oh, Andy," she says, "you are so thought-ful . . . so wonderful . . . so gentlemanly. . . ."

"You forgot handsome," I say.

"And handsome," she says.

"And manly," I say.

"And manly," she says.

"And strong," I say.

"Be serious," she says.

"I was being serious," I say.

She stares at me.

"Before we go any further, I have to ask you a question," she says.

"Anything," I say. "Ask me anything you want."

"Promise me you will answer truthfully, my darling," says Lisa.

"I promise," I say.

She leans forward and whispers into my ear.

Her breath sends shivers through my body that run right down into my toes. I feel dizzy and I hear a roaring sound as the blood rushes to my head. It's so loud I can hardly hear what she's saying. All I can hear is a roaring sort of grinding sound.

Lisa pulls away from me.

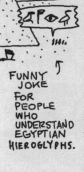

FUNNY JOKE FOR PEOPLE WHO UNDERSTAND EGYPTIAN HIEROGLYPHS.

75

She's studying my face.

"Well?" she says.

"Well what?" I say.

"What's your answer?"

"What was the question?" I say.

"I said," she says, raising her voice above the roar, "did you remember to put the trash out?"

"The what out?" I say.

"The trash!" she screams.

The trash? The trash? What trash?

Oh no — the trash!!!

Suddenly, the sun goes behind a cloud and the street around us is alive with rats — Lisa's hair turns to cobwebs, the skin peels off her face, and she crumbles into a crumpled mummylike heap on the sidewalk. I scream. The whole street dissolves — Lisa disappears. I open my eyes. The room's full of light. How could that be? I look across at the clock. It's 7:30 A.M. I must have fallen asleep! The room is full of the roar and grind of the garbage truck out in the street. And my finger is throbbing. I forgot to cut the string off. But even worse — I forgot to put the trash out!

I jump off the bed and charge out of the room. Luckily, I'm wearing my X-men pajamas.

76

I can run faster when I'm wearing them. I leap down the stairs in one huge bound and sprint for the back door.

I grab the trash can. It's heavy — feels like it weighs at least a thousand pounds — but luckily it's a wheelie trash can. I tip it backward and run as fast as I can with it down the drive-way — just in time to see the garbage truck turn the corner at the bottom of the hill and disappear.

Aaggh!

Dad's going to kill me!

Mom's going to kill me!

If they don't die from the bubonic plague first, that is.

I have to get this trash can emptied . . . and there's only one way to do it.

The garbage truck can't be that far away. They have to stop all the time. And I'm a very fast runner when I need to be.

I take off down the hill.

Or rather, the wheelie trash can takes off down the hill and drags me along with it. If it wasn't for the stink, this would be quite a fun ride. But at the bottom of the hill, the ground levels out and I have to start pushing. I turn left up the next hill.

I can't do it!

It's too hard.

The can is too heavy.

The hill is too steep.

Then I remember the rats.

I think of all the people in the neighborhood who are going to die because I forgot to empty the trash can. Little innocent children — still sleeping — oblivious to their fate. Oblivious to the fact that they are going to be deprived of life because I can't even remember a simple thing like putting the trash out on trash night. The fate of the neighborhood depends on me. I have to go faster.

I bend over and put every bit of strength I have into pushing the can up the hill. I'm going at such an angle that the lid of the can flips back and whacks me in the head. It's a blow that would have knocked anyone else out, but not me. I've got a very hard head. I flip the lid back and keep pushing. Nothing can stop me.

The roaring of the garbage truck is louder now. I'm getting closer. I crest over the top of the hill and see it less than a hundred yards away.

"Stop!" I yell. "Stop! You forgot one!"

There are two men in fluorescent yellow vests running alongside the truck. They pick up the last two trash cans in the street and put them on the tray at the back. It lifts the cans up and empties the trash into the top of the truck.

I'm pushing the can down the hill as fast as I can.

The men put the empty cans on the side of the road and jump back onto the truck to ride to the next street.

"No!" I yell. "Please stop!"

One of them sees me coming and calls out to the driver.

The truck stops and I run up to it with my bin.

"Well, if it isn't one of the X-men!" says one of the men.

"You forgot this one," I say, panting hard. "From the next street."

"Forgot it?" he says. "That's not possible. Are you sure it was on the street when we went past?"

"Yes," I lie. This is another one of those situations where dishonesty is the best policy. It's a lie that could save many lives.

He looks at the other guy.

ONE FINE
TRASH-
CAN DAY.

"Did you forget this one?"

"Nope," says the other one. "I would have seen it."

"Sorry, X-man," says the first guy. "If it had been there, we would have got it."

"Are you saying you don't believe me?" I say.

"I'm not saying anything, buddy," he says. "I'm just saying we can't take it. If it's not outside the house, then we're not permitted to empty it. For all I know, you could be from out of our area — you could be trying to dump your trash illegally."

"But I'm not!" I say. "Why would I want to do that?"

"You'd be surprised what people try," he says, thumping the side of the truck. "Okay, Mac!"

The truck takes off again and the man jumps up on the back.

I watch helplessly as the truck turns into the next street.

But I don't give up that easily.

I know a shortcut through to the next street.

All I have to do is take the trash can through, put it into position, and hide. They'll empty it just like a regular can.

I run down the hill a bit farther and then

BURP! 80

turn right into an alleyway. I push the trash can for all I'm worth and within seconds I'm there.

Up in the distance, I can see the yellow flashing lights of the truck. They've only just turned onto the street. They're still too far away to see me.

Good.

I push the trash can across the opening of the lane and head toward the curb, but the can hits the gutter and lurches sideways.

I lose control and it hits the ground, spilling trash everywhere.

I can't believe what I'm seeing.

Half of the stuff from our garage is lying on the road. Mom and Dad must have cleaned out another closet. I hate it when they do that. They've thrown out some really good stuff. And some of it's mine. My old water wings. A house I made out of matchsticks. And my electric racing car set! I know the controls are missing, pieces of the track are broken, and the cars have lost all their wheels, but that's no reason to throw out a perfectly good electric racing car set!

LIFTED BY A SWARM OF HOUSEFLIES, TRASH PUCKY ROSE UP INTO THE SKY.

I'd better check that there's nothing else of mine in there. I stand the trash can up and look inside.

Oh no. I don't believe it!

She's thrown away the most valuable thing I own in the world — my faithful bath-and-shower companion — my rubber duck! I can see its little yellow beak peeking out from under the trash.

I look up.

The garbage truck is about halfway along the street. I've got just enough time to get my duck and then scram.

"Don't worry!" I say. "I'll save you!"

I lean down into the can, but I can't reach. It's right at the bottom.

I have to lean farther over.

Uh-oh.

Too far!

I fall into the can, headfirst into something squishy and smelly. It doesn't taste too good, either.

And what's worse, I can't move.

I can't get up.

The roaring of the truck is getting louder.

I kick my legs to try to make the can fall over so I can wriggle out.

But my kicking is useless.

All it does is make the lid of the can fall shut on top of me.

Now I'm trapped.

And nobody knows I'm in here!

The truck is right beside me. I can hear it. I feel the can roll off the curb and land on the pavement with a bump. I think it's being put on the tray. I'm rising into the air. It's just like being in an elevator, except much smellier.

I'm yelling my head off but it's no use. They can't hear me over the noise of the truck.

I clutch my duck. The trash can tips upside down and we are dumped into the back of the truck with all the other garbage.

The stink!

The stench!

The horror!

This has got to be the most disgusting thing that's ever happened to me.

I'm being churned around with all the trash. I try to scream but I get a mouthful of used tissues. Everything is a blur as can after can of fresh, rotting garbage is dumped on top of me. Moldy vegetables, putrid fish, and disposable diapers . . . I come face-to-face with a dead cat, but only for a moment — the churning just won't stop. Every time I catch my breath and work my way to the top of the pile a new can-load knocks me down and the churning continues.

ALSO FOUND IN ANDY'S GARBAGE TRUCK.

STEPHANIE FROM DOWN THE ROAD.

MR. SMITH'S FALSE LEG.

STATUE OF LIBERTY.

MR. SMITH'S THREE REAL LEGS.

THE SYMPTOMS OF BUBONIC PLAGUE.

YOUR FEET SWELL UP AND TURN INTO CATS.

WHEN EVER YOU SNEEZE, YOUR HANDS DROP OFF.

YOUR HEAD BECOMES LOOSE.

YOUR MOTHER PUTS YOU OUT ON GARBAGE NIGHT.

WAK!

I've got to get out of here!

I've saved the neighborhood, but I'm going to die!

I'll get bubonic plague.

I think I can feel it coming on already.

Dad's right.

There is nothing funny about being up to your knees in trash — and when it's over your head, it's even unfunnier.

What a pity I won't live to tell him that.

Because I can't fight it anymore.

I'm going to die, suffocated in garbage.

I press my rubber duck to my chest, close my eyes, and prepare for the end.

That's weird.

Everything has gone quiet.

The churning has stopped.

Maybe there's still hope.

I dig my way up out of the trash toward the light.

I push my head through a load of moldy bread, empty dog food cans, and used kitty litter.

But I don't care. I can see the sky!

I raise my duck above my head.

"We're going to make it," I say.

My duck quacks with joy.

HMMM RUBBISH.

I squirm and wriggle the rest of my body out from under the trash until I'm sitting on top of it all.

I wipe the slime from my eyes and look around.

We're traveling along a main road. The truck is obviously full, and they're headed back to the landfill to empty it. I've got to get out before that happens. I don't want to spend the rest of my life as landfill.

We pull up at a set of traffic lights.

This is my chance to escape.

I climb down over the back of the truck onto the platform, and just as the truck starts moving again, I jump clear. I hit the ground running, trip, and roll into the gutter.

Ouch.

It hurts, but it's better than being in a garbage truck any day.

"Are you all right?" says a voice.

A beautiful voice.

The voice of an angel.

I must be dead.

The bubonic plague got me after all, and I've gone to heaven.

But there's something familiar about that voice.

TRASH FASHION.

HALF SKIN OF WATERMELON HAT.

OLD CHICKEN BONE EAR ORNAMENT.

OLD SLICED MEATLOAF BIKINIS.

PEA AND HAM SOUP AND KITTY LITTER HAIR GEL.

I open my eyes.

It's Lisa.

Lisa Mackney looking down at me.

".Andy?" she says.

"Lisa?" I say. "When did you die?"

"Die?" she says. "What are you talking about? We arranged to meet, remember?"

I sit up.

I look around.

This is not heaven. This is hell.

I'm outside the park.

Right where I said I would meet Lisa.

I'm right on time, but everything else is wrong. As wrong as it possibly could be.

There she is, looking clean and fresh and princesslike, her soft hair shining in the morning sun. And here I am, sitting in the gutter in my pajamas, covered in trash, surrounded by flies, clutching my rubber duck.

"I should have known you weren't serious," she says, pinching her nose and backing away from me. "I should have known it was all a joke."

"No, it wasn't!" I say, getting up and stepping toward her. A big slimy chunk of maggot-infested meat slides off my shoulder and plops on the ground in front of her.

She puts her hand over her mouth and takes another step back.

"Keep away from me!" she says. "You . . . you . . . stink!"

I step toward her — kitty litter, cigarette butts, and broken eggshells fall from my clothes and hair as I move.

She turns and runs.

I watch her. The girl I love. Running away from me in disgust.

What was supposed to be the best morning of my life has turned out to be the worst.

And the worst thing about it is that she's never going to want to kiss me now. All that practice on the mirror for nothing.

But at least I got the trash out. At least the neighborhood is safe once more from the bubonic plague.

There's no telling how many lives I've saved.

Not to mention my rubber duck.

Perhaps all is not lost, after all.

I'm going to go home, cut this stupid string off my finger, and have a long shower. A really long shower. I might even use some more of that air freshener — it was pretty strong. Then I'll go to school and explain everything to Lisa.

WEIRD MOMENTS

YOU DON'T WANT TO KISS ME, I'M COVERED IN TRASH.

YOU'RE RIGHT, I DON'T WANT TO KISS YOU.

BUT I'D LOVE THE SLIMY SLICE OF MEAT ON YOUR NOSE.

I'm sure she'll understand. In fact, I can see it now.

When she hears about what I've done, she'll realize what a hero I am. She'll apologize for saying that I stink. She'll beg me to forgive her. I will, of course. And then we'll kiss.

It's lucky I did all that practice on the mirror, after all.

88

Uh-oh!

But, Mom," I say. "I can't look after them. I'm busy."

"Busy?" says Mom. "Busy doing what? Watching television?"

"It's a very important program," I say. "We have to watch it for school."

Mom comes into my room.

I quickly change the channel.

"I saw that!" she says. "Since when did cartoons become important programs?"

"Ever since they were first invented," I say. "But fine. If you don't want me to do my homework, then I won't. I'll fail. I'll drop out. I'll become a full-time babysitter."

"Oh come on," says Mom. "It's just for half an hour. They won't give you any trouble."

I groan.

"Are you kidding?" I say. "They're psychos!"

"Don't be ridiculous," says Mom. "Look at them. They're lovely little girls."

She points toward the kitchen. The girls are sitting at the table having a tea party with their dolls.

"Yeah, they're lovely when you're around," I say, "but it's just an act. As soon as you leave the room, they go crazy."

Mom rolls her eyes and picks up her car keys.

"That's enough, Andy," she says. "I'm not *asking* you — I'm *telling* you. You're looking after them and that's that."

FROM PG. 74.

DR. WOMKLE SAYS "MY DREAM DE-NEBULIZER REALLY WORKS!"
FOR A FREE HOME TRIAL, SEE PG. 151.

The girls — my cousins — have been here for three days now and I'm almost out of my mind. They have been messing up and breaking stuff all over the house, and I've been getting the blame. Mom is looking after them while my aunt is in the hospital having a baby. I wish she'd hurry up and have it. The sooner these kids are out of this house the better.

"Don't leave me here with them, Mom," I say. "Please, I beg you. . . ."

"Bye-bye," she calls to the girls, ignoring me. "I'm going out for a while but Andy will look after you, won't you, Andy?"

She fixes me with an icy glare. I know what that look means. It means that I'd better take very good care of the girls . . . or else.

"Bye-bye," call the girls. They wave and smile so sweetly that, for a moment, I almost believe they are completely innocent, normal little girls.

Mom leaves.

I go to the living room window and watch her car back out of the driveway and drive away down the hill.

I look at the girls.

They're still having their tea party.

So far, so good. Maybe this won't be so bad after all.

I sit back down in front of the TV and change the channel back to my cartoon. Luckily, I haven't missed too much. The mouse is still chasing the cat around, hitting him on the head with an enormous hammer. That poor cat. He never wins. He always gets clobbered. Uh-oh. Now the mouse has a box of matches. He sets the cat's tail on fire.

Wow. That's so realistic I can practically smell the smoke.

Wait a minute.

I *can* smell smoke.

HOW TO IDENTIFY NASTY LITTLE GIRLS:

1. EVIL, CLOSE-TOGETHER EYES.

2. NASTY POINTY NOSE.

3. RAZOR-SHARP FANGS.

4. DOLLY IN ONE HAND, AX IN THE OTHER.

That's not coming from the TV. It's coming from the kitchen. And what's that racket? There's all this banging and clattering. I don't think the girls are playing tea party anymore.

I jump up and run to the kitchen.

There's a haze of blue smoke and the smell of burning rubber.

Jemima's standing up on a chair next to the counter with a fork in her hand, which she's about to stick into the top of the toaster.

"NO!" I say.

She turns around.

"But it's stuck," she says, completely unaware of how close she is to being electrocuted. "It's burning."

"Just leave it," I say, moving toward her. "I'll do it."

"I can do it myself," she says.

"NO!" I scream.

But it's too late. She plunges the fork into the toaster.

I stop. I can't touch her. She must have 220 volts flowing through her body. The electricity might go from her to me.

But I can't just leave her there.

Maybe if I put rubber dishwashing gloves on . . .

p.101

"Got it!" says Jemima, turning to me with something black and smoking on the end of her fork. It doesn't look like toast — it's a dish-washing sponge.

"See," she says. "I told you I could do it my-self."

"But . . . how . . . what . . ." I stutter, "why didn't you get electrocuted?"

"Because I turned the switch off and pulled out the plug first, you dum-dum," she says. "Everybody knows to do that."

"And what were you doing burning a sponge anyway?" I say.

"It's not a sponge," she says, talking to me like I'm stupid. "It's toast for my tea party."

"It's not toast," I say. "It's a sponge and it smells disgusting!"

Something clatters to the floor behind me. I turn around.

Eve has her dolls lined up against the wall and is throwing knives at them.

"And what do you think you're doing?" I say.

"I'm playing circus," she says.

"Well cut it out," I say. "You're not allowed to do that!"

"Who says?" says Eve.

"I say!"

RUBBER DISHWASHING GLOVES AS A FASHION ACCESSORY.

AT WEDDINGS.

AT PARTIES.

GRADUATIONS.

FUNERALS.

ARE YOU LISTENING TO ME?

"You're not the boss of us," she says, throwing another knife at her doll. The knife misses the doll and takes a chunk of plaster out of the wall.

"Yeah, you can't tell us what to do," says Jemima, throwing the fork she was using on the toaster at me.

I duck. The fork flies over my head.

"Right," I say. "You're in big trouble!"

The girls giggle and run out of the kitchen. I run after them but they're gone. I can't see them anywhere. I walk through the living room to the foot of the stairs.

CRASH!

A chess and checkers set lands at the bottom of the staircase. Chess pieces and checkers go flying all over the floor.

I look up.

A game of Monopoly crashes down on my head. Houses and hotels go everywhere. Monopoly money flutters down around me.

Jemima and Eve are hanging off the banister. They're smiling and looking very pleased with themselves.

"Get down here and pick this all up!" I yell.

They just laugh.

"Now!" I say.

I'M TALKING TO YOU.

I start to climb up the stairs.

Jemima pulls a picture off the wall and throws it at me.

I reach out and grab it as it flies through the air. It's a photo of me when I was a little boy. I look like such a nice little kid — not an out-of-control brat — not like them.

I put the picture down and start up the stairs again. But Jemima opens the door of a display case hanging on the wall. Mom keeps her crystal animal collection in there.

"No, Jemima!" I say. "Don't touch that! They're Mom's!"

Too late.

She flings a small sparkly object at me.

I catch it. It's a little crystal mouse. Mom treasures those stupid animals. If anything happens to them, I'll be in big trouble. Even bigger trouble than if anything happened to the girls.

Eve grabs one as well and throws it.

I catch it in my other hand.

"No more," I plead. "No more! I've got no hands left!"

Jemima smiles and then lobs a third one.

I watch as it arcs through the air toward me.

This is the greatest challenge of my life. But I have to do it.

MR. SCRIBBLE CLIMBS THE STAIRS.

95

NOT YOU!

I position myself underneath it, tilt my head back and open my mouth as wide as I can.

The little crystal animal drops onto my tongue. Safe and sound. All that practice throwing pieces of food up into the air and catching them in my mouth at the dinner table has finally paid off.

The girls stand at the top of the stairs and giggle.

"I'm going to kill you!" I scream, although with my mouth full it sounds more like "WYMEGWANAILLOO."

I spit the crystal animal out of my mouth and put it and the other two in my pocket.

I look up toward Eve and Jemima but they're gone. No doubt to find something else to throw.

I run up the stairs.

I look in my room.

They're not there.

I check Jen's room.

They're not there, either.

I look in Mom and Dad's room and the bathroom, but there's no sign of them.

Where can they be?

I check under all the beds, in all the closets, and behind all the curtains.

YOU!

They're gone.

Vanished.

"Eve! Jemima!" I yell. "Where are you?"

"Here!" they call.

That's weird.

Sounds like they're outside.

But they couldn't be outside.

Could they?

Yes, they could!

I look at the window.

I feel sick.

I can see a row of tiny fingertips lined up neatly along the windowsill.

They're hanging outside the house!

Hanging from the second floor!

I rush across to the window. I look down at them.

"You can't catch us," sings Eve. "You can't catch us."

"Girls," I say, "this is not a joke. You could kill yourselves."

"Don't get your knickers in a knot," says Jemima. "We're just hanging out the window."

"You're just about to die!" I say.

I brace my legs against the wall underneath the window, reach out, and grab Eve's wrist with one hand and Jemima's wrist with the other.

PLACE TO HIDE IN THE BATHROOM.

HEE HEE

97 ME?

Got them!

Now all I have to do is pull them in. But they're heavier than they look. As I try to lift them up, it's hard to keep my feet on the floor.

"You're hurting my arm!" says Jemima.

"Shut up!" I say. "I'm trying to save you."

"Uh-oh!" says Eve. "You told Jemima to shut up."

"You shut up, too!" I tell her.

"Uh-oh," they both say.

I struggle some more, but it's hopeless. I'm not pulling them in — they're pulling me out!

I can't do it.

I'm bent over double, already half out the window, and I can feel my knees scraping against the window ledge.

In a few moments, we're all going to fall!

Not that the girls seem to care.

They're giggling and kicking their feet as they dangle in the air.

I hear a clanging noise.

What's that?

"Hey, there's a pipe here," says Jemima.

She's right.

Her feet are almost touching a drainpipe that runs along the outside of the house. It juts out a little way from the wall. If I can just lower them onto it, then I can leave them there while I go and get the ladder.

"Can you stand on it?" I say.

"Sure," she says.

I lower Eve onto the pipe as well.

"Now I'm going to let go," I say. "I want you to stand on the pipe and lean into the wall. Stay there until I get the ladder! Don't move."

Jemima starts bobbing and tapping her foot on the pipe.

"DON'T MOVE!" I yell.

"You're so bossy," says Eve.

I sigh.

"Please don't move," I say. "It's for your own good."

That's the trouble with babysitting little kids. If they hurt themselves, it's the babysitter who gets the blame. It's not fair. Babysitting stinks.

I pull myself back in through the window. I've got to be quick. If they fall, I'm going to be in more trouble than I've ever been in in my whole life.

I sprint downstairs and through the kitchen. It's a big mess. Knives all over the floor.

I slip on one and go skating across the room headfirst into the fridge.

Ouch.

I pick myself up and stagger outside.

I check the side of the house.

But the girls are not there.

I'm too late.

I feel sick.

I look down at the ground under my window, expecting the worst.

But they're not there, either.

CRASH!

A roof tile shatters on the ground beside me.

I look up.

Eve and Jemima are standing on the roof.

"What are you morons doing up there?" I say.

"Uh-oh," says Eve. "You said a rude word. You'll get in trouble."

"Not as much trouble as you're already in!" I say. "I told you to stay put until I got the ladder!"

"We thought you weren't coming," says Jemima. "So we climbed up the pipe."

Eve bends down, picks up a roof tile, and throws it at me.

PLAYING WITH
FLUFFY RABBITS
CAN BE
DANGEROUS.

I step back. It shatters at my feet.

"Hey!" I say. "Cut it out!"

"You can't stop us!" says Jemima. "You're not the boss."

100

HEY,
I ASKED
FIRST.

"We'll see about that," I say.

I run to the garage. The ladder is stuck be-hind a stack of folding chairs and old paint cans. I move them all out of the way and carry it outside.

I lean the ladder up against the house and climb up on the roof.

The girls are gone.

But that's impossible.

"Eve?" I call. "Jemima? Where are you?"

I walk up the roof to the highest point.

I can't see them.

How could they not be there?

Unless they climbed back down the pipe.

Those girls are unstoppable.

I walk back down the roof and get onto the ladder.

I'm climbing back down when I hear gig-gling.

I look down.

The girls are standing at the bottom of the ladder.

Uh-oh.

"Now, Eve!" yells Jemima.

They both pull the ladder out from the side of the house so it's standing straight up in the air.

101

"No!" I yell as the ladder tips backward, and I go crashing into the garden.

I hear the girls laughing hysterically. I push the ladder off me and struggle to my feet, just in time to see Eve running down the driveway.

"Eve!" I yell.

She looks up at me, laughs, and keeps running.

I run after her but she's already rounding the corner at the bottom of the hill.

I have to catch her. There's a busy intersection at the bottom of the hill. It's really dangerous. And I should know. I nearly got killed going through it in a baby carriage once.

I see Jemima's pink bicycle lying on the lawn.

I don't really like the idea of riding a tiny pink girl's bike down the hill, but it's my only hope.

I pick up the bike, jump on it, and start pedaling as hard as I can. My knees are practically hitting my chin. I feel like an idiot.

"Nice bike!" yells a kid from the side of the road. "Pink really suits ya!"

This is embarrassing. My face is burning. I just hope Lisa Mackney doesn't see me.

Despite how awkward it is to ride the bike, I'm gaining on Eve. I catch up and then swing

DR. HAMISH
MCFLOGGIT'S
BRILLIANT
INVENTION,
THE HALF
LADDER.

the bike around in front of her and skid to a stop.

"Gotcha!" I say, grabbing her arm.

But she pushes me away with her other hand. I lose my balance on the bike and fall over.

She runs back up the hill.

I pick myself and the bike up, and limp back up the hill, dragging the bike behind me.

I get back to the house. I'm completely out of breath, my leg hurts, and Eve is nowhere to be seen.

I open the front door and walk in.

I can hear screaming.

It's coming from the living room.

I can't believe what I'm seeing.

Jemima is hanging on to the overhead fan and swinging around.

I've got to hand it to her. Even I've never thought of doing that.

Beside her is a stack of furniture — a stool on top of a chair on top of the glass-topped coffee table — and on top of the swaying stack is Eve. She's poised, her arms outstretched, trying to grab on to the fan as well.

"Don't do it!" I yell, diving toward her. "You'll break it!"

Too late.

Eve jumps. She misses the fan and ends up holding on to Jemima's waist.

I go crashing into the stack of furniture. It collapses around me. The chair falls onto the coffee table and smashes the glass.

Jemima is swinging around on the fan, with Eve hanging off her.

"Wheee!" screams Eve. "This is fun!"

ONE FINE DAY AT THE ELDERLY CITIZENS CLUB.

I run underneath them to try and pull Eve off. I grab her legs, but she won't let go.

There's a cracking noise.

Eve screams.

Jemima screams.

I scream and watch in horror as the fan is wrenched from the ceiling.

The girls come crashing down on top of me.

Without thinking, I put my arms around them and roll us all out of the way.

The fan crashes down onto the carpet, right where we were just lying. The living room is covered in white dust and rubble.

These girls are really out of control.

I've got to stop them before they wreck the whole house.

But how?

WELL! WHO ARE YOU?

ME?

They won't listen to me. They only behave in front of adults.

That's it!

I have to disguise myself as an adult.

And I've got just the thing.

"If you don't stop misbehaving right now I'm going to go and tell Mr. Paddywhack!" I yell.

"Who's that?" they say in unison.

"He's a very scary man!" I say. "And he hates naughty children. He's going to make you behave yourselves!"

"He sounds stupid," says Jemima.

"All right," I say. "That does it! I'm going to get Mr. Paddywhack right now!"

Mr. Paddywhack is this crazy character I made up for a school concert last semester. I dressed up in a white lab coat, a wig made out of the top of an old mop, a yellow hard hat and a diving mask, and I held a tennis racquet in each hand. It was funny because all the little kids were really scared of me — they thought I was going to whack them with my racquets. That's how I came up with the name.

I go up to my room. My costume is still sitting at the bottom of my wardrobe.

I put on the lab coat, the mop wig, the yellow hard hat, and the diving mask.

I get two tennis racquets from the hall closet. I'm not really going to hit them, of course. I'm just going to give them a scare.

I come barreling down the stairs like a madman, waving the racquets above my head.

Jemima and Eve are jumping on the couch.

"I SMELL TWO NAUGHTY CHILDREN!" I yell. "AND I'M GOING TO WHACK THEM!"

"No, you're not," says Jemima, studying my face closely.

"OH, YES I AM!" I yell.

WHY ARE
THERE NEVER
MECHANICAL
BIRDS IN
STORIES
LIKE THESE?

"No, you're not," says Jemima. "You're not even real. You're just Andy dressed up in a stupid wig and hat."

"I'M MR. PADDYWHACK!" I bellow.

"Where's Andy then?" says Jemima.

"He's . . . he's . . ." I say. I didn't expect this question.

"You don't know where he is," says Jemima, "because *you're* Andy!"

Jemima jumps up from the couch and grabs the racquets out of my hand. I try to get them back but she's too fast. She hands one to Eve.

"Whack him!" she says.

Eve whacks me in the leg with the racquet.

106 ...THE MECHANICAL BIRD.

"Ouch!" I yell.

Jemima whacks me on the butt.

"Take that, Mr. Paddywhack!" she squeals.

Eve whacks me on the foot with the edge of the racquet.

I'm getting out of here. I can't take any more.

I start running.

They chase me.

I run out of the living room, into the kitchen, and down the hall. But I can't shake them. They're hot on my heels. I run back into the living room, through the kitchen, and out into the hall again. I run around and around, trying to get away from them. They're maniacs.

I run so fast that I almost run past them. It's hard to tell who's chasing whom.

"COME HERE!" I roar.

The girls look over their shoulders, startled to see me so close. They squeal. I lean forward and snatch the racquets from them.

Fantastic! For the first time today something has gone my way!

"NOW I'VE GOT YOU," I yell, as we run down the hallway. "PREPARE FOR A WHACK-ING!"

"Andy! What on earth do you think you're doing?"

COUCH WARS.

COUCH WE NEED YOU, THE WORLD IS UNDER ATTACK!!

COUCH CLIMBS TO THE TOP OF THE HIGHEST MOUNTAIN

STOP ALL THIS...

BUT BEFORE HE COULD SAVE THE WORLD...

HE WAS STOLEN BY TWO COUCH THIEVES.

Mom is standing in front of us.

When did she get home? I didn't hear her come in.

"Help!" screams Jemima.

"Help!" screams Eve.

They run to Mom and hug her legs.

"Save us!" screams Jemima. "Andy's gone crazy!"

"I haven't gone crazy," I say. "They have!"

"What do you mean by dressing up and scaring the girls like this?" says Mom, her arms around them, trying to comfort them. "I ask you to look after them and I come home and find you chasing them and threatening to hit them with tennis racquets!"

"*They* were chasing *me*!" I say.

I can see Mom looking around the living room, taking in the destruction. The stool and the chair lying on top of the broken coffee table, the wrecked fan, and the chunks of ceiling all over the floor.

"I suppose you're going to tell me all this is the girls' fault as well?" says Mom.

"Yes!" I say. "It is. I tried to stop them. In fact, I saved their lives."

Mom snorts.

"Don't make it worse by lying," she says.

SORRY, PAL...

She strokes the girls' heads. "Are you all right? You poor darlings. What happened?"

"We were just trying to have our tea party," says Jemima, sniffling, "and he came into the kitchen and started bossing us around."

"He wouldn't let me play with my dolls," says Eve.

"But," I say. "She was . . ."

"Then he held us out of his bedroom window," says Jemima. "And he hurt my arm."

"And he said rude words," says Eve.

"But," I say. "They were . . ."

"He left us on the roof!" says Jemima.

"Not exactly," I say. "I was . . ."

"He swung on the fan and broke it!" says Jemima.

"And he broke the table, too," says Eve.

"No, I didn't," I say.

"You did!" says Jemima. "It was your fault."

"Well, it was sort of my fault," I say, "but . . ."

"Then he dressed up as that scary man and chased us around the house," sobs Jemima.

"And he tried to hit us with tennis racquets," wails Eve.

Gee. I've got to hand it to them. Those girls are the best truth-twisters in the world. They're

THE DEATH OF A CEILING FAN.

THE END.

BUT, I'M THE MECHANICAL BIRD.

pretty good at fake crying, too. They're even starting to make *me* feel sorry for them.

They're standing there with their sweet innocent faces and big tearstained eyes. I don't stand a chance. There is nothing I can say. No way is Mom going to believe the real truth.

Poor Mom. I feel sorry for her, too.

I think the full extent of the damage is beginning to dawn on her. She's just staring into the living room, shaking her head.

"Andy, how could you?" she says. "The place is a mess. Everything is wrecked!"

I wish there was something I could say. Something I could do that would make her feel better.

Hang on! There is!

"No, Mom," I say. "Not *everything*!"

"Well, it certainly looks that way to me," she says.

"But I saved these," I say. "Your crystal animals. Look."

I put the tennis racquets down and reach into my pocket.

That's funny.

I thought I put three in there but it feels like a lot more.

I hold out my hand.

110

"Uh-oh," says Jemima.

"Uh-oh," says Eve.

"Well?" says Mom, bending down to pick up one of the tennis racquets. "What have you got to say for yourself?"

I look down at the shattered crystal in my hand.

"Uh-oh," I say.

Pinch

anny is in my bedroom, pressing his face up against my goldfish bowl, staring intently at my new goldfish. He's got his hand above Goldie's bowl.

"Here fishy, fishy, fishy," he says, as he follows Goldie around with his fingers.

"Danny," I say. "Quit it."

"Did you know this guy in Texas in 1970 swallowed two hundred and twenty-five live goldfish?" he says. "It's the world record."

"Shush!" I say. "Goldie might hear you!"

"Don't be stupid," says Danny. "Goldfish can't hear anything — they're underwater!"

"It doesn't matter whether they can hear you or not," I say. "Goldfish are very sensitive. They pick up on your vibes. Especially Goldie."

"What do you think it would be like to have a live goldfish in your stomach?" says Danny. "Do you think you'd be able to feel it swimming around and around inside you?"

"I'm warning you, Danny," I say.

But he's not listening.

He dips his hand into the bowl and grabs Goldie. He tips his head back and dangles her above his mouth.

"That's not funny!" I yell. "Put her back!"

Danny just laughs.

He lowers Goldie until she's almost touching his lips.

He's going to do it. He's really going to do it. I've got to stop him.

I throw myself across the room, but I'm too late.

Danny drops Goldie into his mouth and swallows her. In one gulp. Whole.

"Hey!" I say, pushing him in the chest. "You ate my goldfish!"

"It was an accident," he says. "It slipped."

"That's a lie and you know it!" I say. "You deliberately ate her!"

"Shush," says Danny. He tilts his head as if listening to a faraway sound.

"Hey," he giggles, "I *can* feel it! It tickles."

I'm so angry I'm shaking. Not only has he swallowed Goldie, he doesn't even care. Well, I'll make him care.

I clench my fist tight and swing at his head, but he steps nimbly to the side and I end up punching the air.

I look at my fist. I look at Danny. He is bouncing around on his tiptoes like a boxer.

"Missed me," he says. "Try again!"

I punch again, but Danny skips out of the way.

"Too slow," he says.

I line him up again.

Then I let fly. And this time I connect.

KAPOW!

Danny's head snaps back.

IT WAS A LUCKY PUNCH!

There's an enormous cracking sound, and the next thing I know, Danny's head is flying across the room toward the window.

It bounces off the glass and splashes down into my fishbowl. His head completely fills the bowl. His distorted face looks out at me, his mouth slowly opening and closing.

This is crazy. It can't be happening. Punching someone can't make their head come off, can it? And even if it could, shouldn't they be

114

OW.

dead? Their headless body shouldn't be staggering around bumping into walls should it?

Because that's what Danny's headless body is doing.

And what's that noise?

It sounds like laughter. But it's horrible laughter. Evil and high-pitched. And it's coming from inside Danny's body.

This is too crazy. I mean his head coming off was crazy, but this is TOO crazy.

I'm getting out of here.

I try to run but I can't lift my feet off the ground. They feel like they're nailed to the floor.

I bend down and try to lift them up with my hands, but they won't budge. The high-pitched laughter is getting louder and louder and louder. . . .

Oh no . . . I don't believe what I'm seeing. . . . Hundreds of mini-Dannys are pouring out of the neck of Danny's headless body.

Wave after wave after wave.

Hundreds of them.

Thousands.

They're pouring out of his neck, down his arms, and leaping to the ground . . . and, worst of all, they're heading toward me. Laughing their tiny heads off.

They're really close to me now. They swarm around my feet and start climbing onto my sneakers.

"Hey!" I say, shaking my foot. "Get off!"

But they don't stop.

They keep leaping. I shake even harder. They fly off and land on the carpet, but immediately regroup and keep trying to climb onto my shoes. It's like standing on an ants' nest. They're getting crazier and crazier. And there are more coming. They keep streaming out of Danny's neck. They're everywhere.

I've got no choice.

I'm not normally a violent person, but I'm going to have to squash them.

I start stomping.

But it doesn't stop them.

As I flatten them they split into two and each mini-Danny becomes two even minier-Dannys. And the minier-Dannys laugh even harder and louder than the mini-Dannys.

They all start leaping onto the bottom of my jeans. They're climbing up my legs like spiders. I've got to stop them. If I don't, they'll be all over me in seconds.

I look around.

There's a can of bug spray on the windowsill. I brought it into my room to use against mosquitoes — I hope it works against mini-Dannys.

I snap the lid off and start spraying my legs.

As the spray hits them, the mini-Dannys fall backward onto the floor, spin around on their backs, and kick their legs in the air.

But it doesn't stop the others from trying.

For every one that I kill, two take its place. And when I kill those two, four more jump on, laughing the whole time. The noise is incredible.

This is so horrible. It can't be happening.

Hang on.

Maybe it's not happening.

Maybe it's just another one of my crazy dreams. I've been having a lot lately.

If it's a dream, then all I have to do is pinch myself and I'll wake up and everything will be fine.

I put the bug spray down on the windowsill and pinch the skin on my forearm. Ouch.

I blink.

The light hurts.

I look around.

GIANT
DANNY

I'm in my bed, drenched in sweat.

At least I hope it's sweat.

What a relief!

It *was* just a dream.

A nightmare.

But at least I'm awake now.

I look over at my fishbowl.

That's strange.

Goldie's missing.

But I only dreamed that Danny swallowed Goldie . . . didn't I? If Goldie's really gone, that means I wasn't dreaming and if I wasn't dreaming, that means that . . . well, I'm not sure what it means. . . .

And why is the room shaking?

Is this an earthquake?

The plaster on the roof above my bed is cracking. A big chunk of it falls onto my bed.

I hear a loud splintering sound. Dust and bits of plaster rain down onto my bed and the room is filled with light.

It's like the roof has been lifted off the house.

Maybe it's not an earthquake. Maybe it's a cyclone.

No!

It's a gigantic Danny!

118

A Danny that towers into the sky.

A Danny that looks as big to me as I must have looked to the mini-Dannys.

He's hideous.

But he's unmistakably Danny.

He tosses the roof away as if it's no heavier than the lid of a shoebox. It crashes to the ground. The whole house shakes.

Danny throws back his head and laughs. An enormous earsplitting laugh that seems to fill the whole world.

He reaches down, picks me up by the collar of my pajama top, and lifts me high into the air. He tilts his head back and holds me above his mouth.

Oh no!

He's going to eat me — just like he ate Goldie!

It is a horrible view from up here.

I can see every filling in his mouth. His big disgusting tongue. I can see every crack and fissure — and there's this yellow gunk all over it. But the worst thing is his breath. It smells like dead fish. And it's blowing all over me.

I don't want to go in there.

I don't want to die.

But there's nothing I can do.

I'm dangling in the air.

And then Danny lets go.

I'm going down, down, down.

Down into the slimy dark-redness of Danny's throat.

It's all around me.

The warm squishy walls.

Pressing.

Squishing.

Digesting.

Digesting!

I've got to get out of here.

I've got to go up.

But I'm going down.

Suddenly the squishing stops.

I fall into a big red cave.

Dark.

Dripping.

Wet.

I land on something squelchy. Everything's sort of wobbly and unsteady. It's like being in a jumping castle that's covered in slime.

I guess this must be Danny's stomach.

What am I saying? I can't be in Danny's stomach.

This can't be real.

I must be dreaming.

That's it. Of course. I'm still in my dream.

Or am I? Is it a dream, or maybe it's some sort of weird hallucination. What if I've gone crazy but I don't know I've gone crazy because not knowing I've gone crazy is part of the craziness? But then the fact that I'm thinking this means that I *must* know I'm crazy so I *can't* be crazy. But how can I be sure that I'm not just dreaming that I'm crazy — or that I'm crazy, and I'm just having a regular dream? I could try pinching myself again, but that didn't really help the first time. That's how I ended up in here. What if I pinch myself and I end up in an even worse dream? I couldn't stand it. This is bad enough.

No.

I'm just going to have to deal with the situation as it is. It's the only way.

I have to find a way out of Danny's stomach. But how?

As my eyes adjust to the dimness, I can see a whole landscape emerge from the gloom around me.

It has a sort of lunar feel — everything is covered in some kind of white powder. It's all over me. I brush myself off and sniff my fingers. I know that smell. It's sherbet! Judging by how much of it is down here, Danny must live on the stuff.

There's a big lake in front of me. I have to be careful. That could be Danny's stomach juices. I crouch down for a closer look. It doesn't look like stomach juices, though. It's sparkling and full of bubbles, like lime soda. I put a finger in and taste a bit. It *is* lime soda!

On the other side of the soda lake there appears to be a snowcapped mountain range. It's not like a normal mountain range, though — it's pink and white and brown. As I peer closely, I can see that it's actually ice cream. And next to it there appear to be hundreds — possibly thousands — of doughnuts. All sitting around in huge piles like stacks of old tires at a junkyard.

No wonder Danny is acting so strange.

He lives on a diet of pure sugar.

Except for the occasional human, that is.

But how am I going to get out?

I look up. There's no way I can climb back up the walls of Danny's throat. They're too slippery. Besides, the opening I fell through must be more than three hundred feet above me. I couldn't reach it even if I tried.

I look all around me.

AND DEEP IN THE CAVERNS OF HIS STOMACH, I MET OLD BEN BUNN, A CASTAWAY. HE TOLD ME MANY STORIES OF HIS YEARS LOST IN DANNY'S STOMACH.

HA HA MISSED!

122

AND THAT!

I see something flashing in the lime soda lake. Something that glitters.

I move toward it.

It's Goldie!

I reach down and pick her up.

"Don't worry, Goldie," I say, slipping her into my pajama pocket. "I'll get us out of here!"

I hear a long low noise in the distance.

It sounds like a foghorn.

I look up. In front of me I can see a tunnel sloping downward.

That could be a way out.

SUDDENLY, IT ROSE BEFORE ME, FOUL AND AWESOME!! THE BODY OF A HUGE CHICKEN LEG AND THE EYE OF A MAN, JUST AS BEN BUNN HAD DESCRIBED IT.

I start running as fast as I can; but as I run farther along the tunnel, it gets darker, the smell gets worse, and the foghorn gets louder.

Uh-oh.

If that's the only way out, then I'd rather stay in.

I run back the way I came.

Perhaps being in Danny's stomach is not so bad after all. At least there's ice cream. And doughnuts. And sherbet. And all that soda. No wonder Danny burps so much.

Actually, it gives me an idea.

When you mix sherbet and ice cream and soda together, it bubbles and froths. If I stirred all this stuff together in Danny's stomach,

OUCH! 123

maybe I could create enough gas to make him burp it — and me — up and out of here.

It's worth a try.

I scrape the sherbet into a big pile and push it into the soda. The lake starts frothing and bubbling.

Good, but no sign of a burp yet.

I grab enormous handfuls of ice cream and add them to the lake.

Better — the froth is building — but still I need more.

I scrape more sherbet and hurl more ice cream.

Eventually the froth starts to overflow the lake. The whole spitting, popping, bubbling mess is out of control. It's all around me.

Suddenly, the stomach is filled with a low rumbling noise. The spongy floor wobbles like jelly. I put my arms out and try to stop myself from falling, but I trip and stumble backward.

I lose my balance, but I don't fall. Instead, I'm swept up in a tornado of burp gas and sucked back up the way I came.

I shoot up the throat at an amazing speed.

I'm going so fast that I miss the turnoff to Danny's mouth and go hurtling up into his nose.

This is very bad.

AS I CLUNG DESPERATELY TO MY PIECE OF TOAST, THE WARNINGS OF BEN BUNN RANG IN MY EARS: "BEWARE THE GIANT SQUID!!!"

MISSED.

If I come flying out at this speed, I could be killed.

But hang on!

I'm flying headfirst into a forest of nostril hairs.

I grab one. Some nostril hair! It's as thick as a piece of rope.

I swing up, hit the wall of Danny's nose, and swing back again. This is even more fun than swinging on the clothesline. I swing back and forth a few times before slowing down and stopping.

Okay, I've avoided death by splattering. Now to get out of Danny's nose safely.

But just as I'm about to let go of the nostril hair, I see a new danger:

Danny's finger!

He's picking his nose!

I climb the nostril hair as far up as I can to try and get out of the giant finger's way, but it's no use. The finger is filling the entire nostril. It's like an enormous battering ram. It's pushing me up against these big rubbery beanbags.

Except they're not beanbags.

And they're not made of rubber.

Erggh. That's disgusting! I'd rather die any other way than this.

THE NOSE-PICKERS GUIDE TO GOURMET FOODS OF THE HUMAN BODY.

SNOT: 4 STAR

EARWAX: STRONG TASTE, BUT RICH IN CALORIES.

BELLY BUTTON LINT: NOT RECOMMENDED.

TOE JAM: A TASTE THAT TAKES SOME GETTING USED TO, BUT WELL WORTH IT.

I'm being pushed deeper and deeper into them. It's getting hard to breathe.

Suddenly, I'm being rocketed forward again — attached to the end of Danny's finger.

I blink as I emerge into the light.

Danny points his finger toward his eyes and studies the end of it. He sees me.

He starts to laugh.

The overpowering stench of his breath almost makes me lose consciousness.

What's he going to do with me?

He's got to let me go now.

Surely he's made me suffer enough.

He moves his finger toward his mouth.

Oh no.

That's disgusting.

I don't mind admitting that I've picked my nose occasionally — well, more than occasionally — practically every day if you want to know the truth — but I've never, ever eaten it. Not on purpose, anyhow. I have my standards.

This is it. I've had all I can take.

I'm going to pinch myself.

Maybe things could get worse. But then again, it's hard to imagine anything worse than being covered in snot and eaten by a giant.

I pinch my arm as hard as I can.

I wake up in my bed.

I check the ceiling.

It's completely intact.

I check the floor.

No mini-Dannys.

So far so good.

Everything appears to be normal.

I check the goldfish bowl to see if Goldie is there. I can see something swimming in it. I suppose that's Goldie but I can't tell exactly. My vision is all blurry. And my eyes are burning.

I focus as hard as I can, but what I'm seeing doesn't make sense.

It's not Goldie . . . it's . . . it's . . . it's me!

A tiny me swimming around and around the bowl.

But that can't be me . . . because I'm here . . . at least I think I'm here. . . .

I look down at my body.

But I'm not me.

I'm a giant goldfish.

Wait! I'm obviously still dreaming . . . I've got to pinch myself again . . . but how do I pinch myself without arms or fingers? All I've got is a couple of useless fins!

I start flipping and flopping and flapping.

Crash.

SO WAS THAT!
127

GANGS OF ANGRY YOUNG VACUUMS WILL OFTEN ATTACK LONE AND DEFENSELESS CLEANING LADIES.

← MR. ANGRY BROOM.

THIS KIND OF BEHAVIOR MUST NOT BE SIMPLY BRUSHED UNDER THE CARPET.

I fall off the bed onto the floor.

There is a knock on the door.

"Help!" I yell. "Help!"

But nothing comes out.

I can't talk. I can only open and close my mouth.

There is another knock.

"Andy?" says Mom. "Are you awake yet?"

That's a very good question. I wish I knew.

The door opens.

Mom walks in.

"Why are you lying on the floor, you silly boy?" she says.

Boy? She called me a boy. That must mean that . . . I look down at my body. I'm not a goldfish anymore. Thank goodness.

"You have a visitor," says Mom.

"Who?" I say.

"Danny," she says.

"No!" I yell. "Not Danny. Keep him away from me!"

But it's too late — he's already in.

I can see his nostrils flaring.

I can see his fingers.

I know where they've been.

"Hi, Andy," he says.

I scream.

MISSED ME.

⁂@*!

"What on earth is the matter with you?" says Mom.

"Matter?" I say. "I'll tell you what's the matter! He ate Goldie . . . then his head came off and a whole army of mini-Dannys attacked me, and then he became a giant and ripped the roof off the house and ate me, and then picked me out of his nose and tried to eat me again. . . ."

Mom and Danny are laughing.

"Sounds like you've been having a bad dream," says Mom. "But you're awake now."

"But am I?" I say. "How can I be sure? Every time I think I'm awake, the dream starts up again!"

"I had one of those once," says Danny. "I kept dreaming I was eating doughnuts. Millions and millions and millions of them. And every time I woke up, I'd just be eating more doughnuts . . . it was really cool."

I scream again.

Mom sits on the side of the bed and strokes my head.

"Calm down, Andy," she says. "You're really awake now."

"I am?" I say.

"Yes," she says. "There's nothing to worry about."

IF YOU SUFFER FROM BAD NIGHTMARES, YOU MIGHT LIKE TO TRY:

DR. WOMKLE'S DREAM DE-NEBULIZER.

FOR FURTHER DETAILS, SEE Pg. 74.

I'M NOT JUST WACKY!

I'M VERY WACKY!!

129

GOT!

But I'm not so sure. Something doesn't feel right.

I look at the goldfish bowl. Goldie's missing!

A bolt of fear shoots down my spine.

I point to an empty bowl.

"If I'm awake," I say, "then where's Goldie?"

Danny steps forward.

"There she is!" he says.

Goldie is flipping around on the carpet. Danny picks her up and puts her back in the bowl.

"There," says Mom. "See? Danny didn't hurt Goldie — he saved her. She must have jumped out of the bowl."

But I'm still scared.

I don't trust Danny.

"I don't know, Mom," I say. "How do we know that he didn't already have her in his stomach and he just burped her up, put her on the carpet, and pretended to save her?"

Danny laughs.

"What are you talking about?" he says.

"That's a very good question, Danny," says Mom, getting up off my bed.

"Don't leave me, Mom!" I plead. "Don't leave me alone with him!"

"Don't be ridiculous," says Mom.

She leaves the room.

Maybe she's right.

Maybe I really am awake.

Maybe the dream really is over.

I look over at Danny.

My stomach drops.

He's pressing his face up against Goldie's bowl. He's got his hand above it and is following Goldie around with his fingers.

"Here fishy, fishy, fishy," he says. "Here fishy, fishy, fishy."

Kittens, Puppies, and Ponies

'm sitting in the gym listening to Mr. Rowe drone on and on. Mr. Rowe is the vice principal. He only gets to conduct whole school assemblies once or twice a year, and when he does, he makes the most of it.

"It's time some of you took a good long look at yourselves in a mirror," says Mr. Rowe. "Ask yourselves if you like what you see. Listen to yourselves speak. Ask yourselves if you like what you hear. There are no such words as *gunna* and *youse*. . . ."

I wish he'd hurry up and get to the most important part. The announcement of the winner of the school short-story competition.

The reason I'm looking forward to this is because the winner is going to be me.

How do I know?

It's simple.

Because I've written a story that is a surefire winner. The judges are going to love it.

I usually write stories full of action, explosions, monsters, and violence. But I never win. The judges always go for the boring sappy stuff. So this year I've decided to give them exactly what they want. I've written the boringest, sappiest story in the world. Plus it has a happy ending. It can't fail.

DANNY THE DUNG BEETLE READS ABOUT HIS FAVORITE CHARACTER: POOH BEAR.

Don't get me wrong.

I'm not proud of this story.

I just wrote it because it's the only way to win the competition. And the only reason I want to win the competition is to impress Lisa Mackney. She is always going on about books and writers and how she wants to be a famous author one day, so I figure the best way to get her to take me seriously is to win the competition.

DANNY THE DUNG BEETLE GETS HIT WITH A MALLET.

When Lisa sees me win the competition, she's going to realize once and for all what a deeply thoughtful, poetic, and sensitive person I really am.

MAKE LOVE NOT WAR

HMM!

133

Danny leans across.

"When am I going to get to read your story?" he whispers.

"DID YOU LIKE MY STORY??"

"I don't think it's really the sort of story you'd like, Dan," I say.

"But that's not fair," says Danny. "I showed you mine. I won't laugh. I promise."

"You really want to read it?" I say.

"Yes!" says Danny.

I pull a copy of my story out of my pocket and pass it to him.

Up until now, I haven't shown it to anybody. I've kept it strictly top secret. I couldn't take the risk that somebody else might steal my idea and try to pass it off as their own.

Danny takes the story. I read it over his shoulder, just to make sure that it's as bad as I remember.

Kittens, Puppies, and Ponies by Andy Griffiths

SAM'S DRAWING OF KITTENS, PUPPIES, AND PONIES.

Once upon a time, there was a magical kingdom called Lovelyville. Everything was lovely in Lovelyville. The people were lovely, the

134

JOY TO THE WORLD

SHE'S RIGHT.

weather was lovely, and the animals were lovely. There were no
horrible spiders, poisonous
snakes, or giant cockroaches.

No. There were none of these
things.

Just lovely animals like kittens, puppies, and ponies. They
played and frolicked and scampered around in the meadows causing no harm to anybody.

One day, one of the kittens
had an idea.

"I know," she said, "let's go
around to all the townspeople
and give them each a big hug!"

"What a good idea!" said a
pony. "We could give them rides
as well!"

"And lick their faces!" said a
puppy.

"Yes!" said the kitten. "Let's
do it right now!"

And so all the animals set
off.

The first house they came to
belonged to Mr. White.

JAZ'S DRAWING OF LOVELYVILLE.

I'M SOOOO CUTE.

135

MORE HUGS

I FEEL ASHAMED

I'M CUTER. (I HAVE BIGGER EYES.)

He opened the door and saw all the kittens, puppies, and ponies of Lovelyville on his doorstep.

"Hello!" said the kitten. "We've come to give you a big hug!"

Mr. White looked at the playful, scampering group — their sleek, well-groomed bodies shining in the morning sun — and his heart was gladdened. The kitten jumped up into his arms and hugged him. The puppy leaped up and licked his face. The pony came forward, and Mr. White climbed onto its back and went for a ride, tears of joy pouring down his face. And the animals didn't stop there. They kept going until they'd hugged and licked and given rides to every last person in Lovelyville.

I'M MR. WHITE, AND I'M SO CUTE YOU COULD RUN ME OVER WITH A STEAMROLLER.

"What a lovely day we've had!" said the kitten.

"Yes," said the puppy. "It's lovely to do lovely things for people."

SMOOCH

136

"Now Lovelyville is even lovelier than ever," said the pony.

And the townspeople gave the kittens, puppies, and ponies three cheers, and everybody ate their vegetables, brushed their teeth, and went to bed early.

The End.

Danny hands the story back to me. He's shaking his head.

"Well," I say, "what did you think?"

Danny takes a deep breath.

"You want the truth?" he says.

"Yes," I say.

"It stinks," says Danny. "I hate it."

"That's good," I say. "If you hate it, then the judges will love it!"

"I wouldn't be so sure about that," says Danny.

"You'll see I'm right," I whisper. "When I win."

"No, that's where you're wrong," says Danny. "Because I'm going to win."

"What?" I say. "With a story about a giant mechanical chicken that goes rampaging through the streets wrecking everything and killing everybody? You'll never win with that. The judges just don't go for all that action stuff."

"How do you know what the judges like?" says Danny.

"Because I've worked it out," I say. "Every year we write stories about killer robots, killer aliens, and killer chickens, right?"

"Yeah," says Danny. "So?"

"And have our stories ever won?" I say.

"No," says Danny.

"Exactly," I say. "The winner is always Tanya Shepherd with some cute story about bunnies or teddy bears or elves. Well, not this year, because I'm going to beat her at her own game."

"Shush!" hisses a teacher standing at the end of our row.

Danny and I sit up in our chairs and look to the front.

But nothing has changed.

Mr. Rowe is still going on and on and on. Blah, blah, blah. I wish he'd hurry up and finish.

I just want to get up there, collect my prize, make Lisa fall in love with me, and get out of here.

Mr. Rowe pauses, clears his throat, and

pauses again, as if he's forgotten what he's saying. He shuffles some sheets of paper and pulls out an envelope.

"And now for the winner of the short-story competition," he says.

At last!

"We received a record number of stories for this year's competition — more than ten, in fact — and the judges had a very difficult time deciding on a winner because they were all of such a high standard. . . ."

That's funny. I would have thought mine was so obviously superior that it would have made the judges' job really easy. Perhaps he's talking about the runner-up.

"However," says Mr. Rowe, "in spite of the difficulty, they have decided on a winner. . . ."

Yes! Me, you gasbag! Just say my name and let me up there on that stage!

". . . but before I announce the winner . . ."

Oh come on! Get on with it!

"I just want to say that as far as I'm concerned, every person who put an entry into the competition is a winner, and whether or not you actually win the competition is not important. The important thing is to have tried. . . ."

In case you're not familiar with Mr. Rowe's

speeches, what he's actually trying to say is that he's going to announce the winner (that's me), and that we're all going to pretend that the losers (that's everybody else) are winners as well. That's so they won't feel so bad about losing, which is quite pointless really because everybody will know that the losers are still the losers and that I, the winner, am still the winner.

"But without any further ado," says Mr. Rowe, opening the envelope and pulling out a small folded piece of paper, "the runner-up of this year's short-story competition is . . . Daniel Pickett for his entry, 'Killer Mechanical Chickens from Outer Space.'"

Huh? I don't believe it. Danny can't win second prize. Not with a story like that. The judges never award prizes to stories about robotic killers from outer space. Especially not if they're chickens. It doesn't make sense. Maybe they just felt sorry for him.

Everybody applauds. Danny stands up, walks to the stage, receives his certificate, and walks back to his seat, his grin as wide as his face.

I lean across and shake his hand.

"Congratulations, Danny," I say. "You

missed out on the top prize, but don't feel bad—you were up against me, after all."

"Thanks," he says.

"And now," says Mr. Rowe, "the moment you've all been waiting for . . . the winner of this year's short-story competition is . . ."

ME!
ANDY GRIFFITHS!
THE BEST!
THE STAR!

Mr. Rowe pauses for dramatic effect and clears his throat.

". . . Tanya Shepherd for her story, 'The Ballerina Princess.'"

I jump out of my seat, my hands clasped above my head in victory, and start heading toward the stage when I realize everybody is laughing. Except for Mr. Rowe. He's frowning. I stop, halfway between my seat and the stage.

"Excuse me, young man," he says. "Is your name Tanya Shepherd?"

Everybody starts laughing again.

It takes me a little while to understand the question.

Tanya? My name's not Tanya. At least I don't think it is.

"Well?" says Mr. Rowe.

I look at Mr. Rowe standing there in front of me.

"No," I say.

"Then sit down, you silly boy," he says.

There's a fresh round of laughter as I turn around and walk back to my seat.

I can't believe what's happened.

Tanya Shepherd has beat me. Again.

She walks up onto the stage and Mr. Rowe presents her with my certificate. It's all happening like a dream. No, not a dream. A nightmare. It's crazy, that's what it is. It's all wrong.

Danny leans across.

"Tough luck," he says, patting me on the arm. "But don't feel too bad about it. Remember what Mr. Rowe said? You're a winner, too, not a loser. You tried."

I pull away my arm.

"That's garbage and you know it!" I say.

"Yeah," says Danny. "I guess you're right. Your story really did stink. You *are* a loser."

He's right.

I shouldn't have tried to write a story that the judges would like. I should have written a story that *I* would like.

In fact, that's exactly what I'm going to do.

After the assembly, we go back to our classroom to get our lunches. Everybody goes outside except me.

I spend half of lunchtime rewriting my story.

I've finished the last sentence when Danny comes into the room.

"Okay, are you ready to hear it?" I say.

"Hear what?" says Danny.

"My story," I say. "I've rewritten it."

"The one about the kittens?" he says. "Why?"

"I've fixed it up."

"Is there any hugging in it?" says Danny.

"No," I say.

"What about face licking?" he says.

"No," I say. "I promise."

"All right," says Danny, sitting down. He doesn't look too happy.

I start reading.

CATE AND ANNA TALK BOOKS.

DO YOU READ BOOKS?

YES, I READ BOOKS.

BOOK

Kittens, Puppies, and Ponies: The TRUE Story by Andy Griffiths

Once upon a time, there was a magical kingdom called Lovelyville. Every-

AND THAT 143 MISSED

(HAND GRENADE.)
(HARD TO DRAW.)

thing was lovely in Lovelyville. The people were lovely, the weather was lovely, and the animals were lovely. There were no horrible spiders, poisonous snakes, or giant cockroaches.

No. There were none of these things.

Just lovely animals like kittens, puppies, and ponies. They played and frolicked and scampered around in the meadows causing no harm to anybody.

One day, one of the kittens had an idea.

"I know," she said, "let's go around to all the townspeople and give them each a big hug!"

"What a good idea!" said a pony. "We could give them rides as well!"

"And lick their faces!" said a puppy.

"Yes!" said the kitten. "Let's do it right now!"

And so all the animals set off.

The first house they came to belonged to Mr. White.

He opened the door and saw all the kittens, puppies, and ponies of Lovelyville on his doorstep.

"Hello!" said the kitten. "We've come to give you a big hug!"

Now the animals didn't know it, but Mr. White was the only unlovely person in Lovelyville, and he had only one thing on his evil mind that morning — who was he going to use to test his new PULVERIZING AND MASHING MACHINE™? He couldn't believe his good luck.

"Well," he said, "what a nice surprise! Won't you all please come inside?"

The animals went inside.

Mr. White shut the door and locked it. He rubbed his hands.

"Prepare to die!" he said. He pulled a cord, and a heavy black curtain parted to reveal his insanely evil PULVERIZING AND MASHING MACHINE™.

JAZ's DRAWING OF PULVERIZING MACHINE.™

PLEASE COME INSIDE.

145

STOP THIS MADNESS.

The animals gasped.

In front of them was a bathtub, and suspended above it were two giant pistons. On the end of one piston was what looked like a giant potato masher, and on the other a giant pitchfork.

The animals were very frightened.

"Who's going to be first?" said Mr. White.

The kitten gulped.

"Take me and let the others go free!" she begged.

"And deprive me of a wonderful morning's entertainment?" said Mr. White. "You must be crazy! I intend to pulverize and mash all of you! And then I will turn my PULVERIZING AND MASHING MACHINE™ to work upon the whole town of Lovelyville! I will not be happy until I have popped off the head of every lovely person, mashed the petals of every lovely flower, and crushed every single lovely thing in this lovely, lovely land!"

146

And on saying this, he reached out and grabbed all the animals, threw them into his machine, and pressed the ON button.

It was incredible. Bits and pieces of kittens, puppies, and ponies went flying everywhere as the twin pulverizers and mashers went to work, and the blood and guts and fur went all over Mr. White and filled up the house and he drowned, and then the house blew apart and a tidal wave of blood and guts flooded out over the whole town, and everybody got drowned and those who didn't got sucked into the PULVERIZING AND MASHING MACHINE™ and got pulverized and mashed — every last lovely person, every last lovely animal, every last lovely vegetable and mineral — all mashed beyond recognition, all pulverized beyond belief, every last bit of loveliness crushed, killed, and destroyed.

And the town was renamed BLOODY-VILLE and nobody ever went there

147

AFTER ALL THAT PULVERIZING AND MASHING I THINK I NEED SOME REALLY LOVELY HUGS!

again because the smell was so bad that anybody who smelled it died instantly.

The End.

I put down the story.

Danny's eyes are wide. His mouth is frozen open. He's staring at me in horror.

"Danny?" I say. "Danny? Are you all right?"

He can hardly talk. I've obviously really freaked him out. He points at me.

"It's just a story, Danny," I say. "It didn't really happen."

I look closer at him.

He's not pointing at me at all. He's pointing over my shoulder.

I turn.

Oh no.

Lisa is standing behind me. She's crying. And not just crying. I mean sobbing. Tears are streaming down her cheeks. She must have heard the whole thing.

"Those poor animals," she sobs. "They didn't deserve that. It was so cruel. Such a cruel, heartless thing to do."

"Um . . . err . . . ah," I stutter. "It's just a story."

I know this is a pathetic answer, but I don't know what else to say. I've blown it. Really blown it.

"Did you write it?" sobs Lisa.

What can I say? She's going to hate me if I admit it's mine. I don't want her to hate me. There's only one thing I can do. Lie.

"No," I say. "It's not my story."

"It's not?" she sobs.

Danny frowns.

"But . . ." he says.

"No!" I say. "I swear on my mother's grave that I didn't write it!"

"But your mother's not dead, is she?" says Lisa.

"My grandmother's grave," I say.

"But she's not dead, either," says Danny. "She lives in Mildura and . . ."

"Well, actually no, Danny," I lie. "I forgot to tell you that she died."

"She was okay last week," says Danny.

"It was very sudden," I say. "She just got sick and died. It happens, you know."

"Oh," says Danny. "I'm sorry."

SORRY,
I CHANGED
MY MIND.

TRIPLE
HMM. 149 WE NEED
TO
UNDERSTAND
EACH
OTHER.

SPEAKING OF GRAVES...

BOBOLES
GONZO FIDO
FLUFFY POOH
FIFI TOTO

WE DON'T HAVE MUCH LUCK WITH PETS.

"So am I," says Lisa.

"Yeah, well, never mind," I say, "but I swear on my grandmother's extremely freshly dug grave that I did not write that story."

"Then if you didn't," says Lisa, "who did?"

I point at Danny.

"It was him!" I say.

Danny looks alarmed.

"Me?" says Danny. "But . . ."

Lisa turns to Danny.

Boy, he's really in for it now. Lisa loves animals.

"That's the saddest story I've ever heard," says Lisa, her eyes shining through her tears. "So sad, so moving . . . so cruel, and yet . . . so beautiful. You're a very talented writer, Danny."

What? She likes it? But she was crying. I thought she hated it! I'll never understand girls.

But I can't tell her that I wrote it now. I can't go back on my lie. Especially when I just swore on my grandmother's grave. I know my grandmother's not really dead, but to admit that would only make me a double liar. The only thing to do is to try to take some of the credit.

"It was my idea," I say. "I helped him."

"Yeah," says Danny. "Andy was a big help. He practically wrote it."

FLUFFY

HERE, SIT DOWN. RELAX.

4x HMM.

150

Lisa shakes her head.

"I'm sure you're just being modest," she says. "You were the runner-up in the school short-story competition after all."

"I helped him with that story, too," I say.

"You did not," says Danny, puffing his chest out. "That was all *my* work."

"No, it wasn't," I say.

Lisa rolls her eyes.

"Quit kidding around, Andy," she says.

Danny looks at me and shrugs.

"Danny," says Lisa. "You know that project we have to do for English where we have to write about our favorite author?"

From Pg. 90

FOR A FREE HOME TRIAL OF DR. WOMKLE'S DREAM DE-NEBULIZER SEE Pg. 183

"Yeah," says Danny. "What about it?"

"Well," she says, "I was wondering if I could do mine on you?"

Danny blushes a deep red.

"I guess so," he stammers.

DR. WOMKLE.

I cough. I splutter. I gag. But they ignore me.

"Great!" says Lisa, opening her notebook. "Can I interview you? I'd love to know where you get your ideas from."

"Well," says Danny, sitting up in his chair and folding his arms. "It's not that hard. You just need some sort of monster. It's not that important what it is. It can be an alien . . . or a robot . . . or even a chicken. It doesn't matter. It just has to be evil and want to destroy everything."

"Like this, you mean?" I say. I raise my arms, roar like a monster, and stomp toward Danny. I'm going to rip him to pieces.

Lisa touches my arm.

"Andy," she sighs, "you are so immature. If you're not interested in learning from someone as talented as Danny, then please go away and leave us in peace."

"Yes," says Danny. "Why don't you run along and play?"

I don't know what to say.

I put my arms down, turn, and shuffle slowly toward the door.

This has got to be the lowest point of my entire life. And that's saying something.

But hold on.

I may have lost the competition.

I may have lost my dignity.

And I may have lost the best chance I've ever had to impress Lisa.

But I'm not a loser.

I'm a winner.

Because now I know exactly what sort of stories Lisa likes.

All I have to do is write another one.

I can't wait to get started on it.

I don't exactly know what's going to happen yet, but I do know it will involve bunnies, lambs, fluffy ducklings, a couple of baby seals, and a maniac driving a steamroller.

She's going to love it.

THERE ARE NEVER ANY STORIES ABOUT HAIRY DUCKLINGS.

THE ADVENTURES OF HARRY HUMAN. BLAH, BLAH, BLAH...

Learn to Read
with Andy

See me jump.

See me run.

See me hop.

It is fun.

See me hop.

See me run.

See me jump.

Fun, fun, fun.

See me jump.

On my bed.

I jump so high,

I bump my head.

On the ceiling.

On the roof.

I hit it hard.

Ouch! Ugh! Oof!

I say a word.

It is bad.

It is rude.

I am glad.

I like to swear.

It is fun.

Bad words, rude words.

Fun, fun, fun.

Hop, hop, hop.

Bump, bump, bump.

Swear, swear, swear.

Jump, jump, jump.

On my tummy.

On my bum.

See me jump.

Fun, fun, fun.

Hear my bedsprings.

Hear them groan.

Hear them squeak.

Hear them moan.

Squeak, squeak, squeak.

Groan, groan, groan.

Creak, creak, creak.

Moan, moan, moan.

This is not good.

This is bad.

Mom will hear.

She'll get mad.

I'll be in trouble.

I'll be sad.

Big trouble,

bad trouble.

Bad, bad, bad.

Oh no! Oh no!

Here she comes.

Oh no! Oh no!

Here comes my mom.

Stomp! Stomp! Stomp!

Down the hall!

I do not like this.

Not at all.

The door flies open.

She's mad as hell.

See her point.

Hear her yell:

"Are you jumping
on your bed?

You stupid boy!

You'll crack your head!

I've told you once.

I've told you twice.

It is not good.

It is not right.

You must not jump

upon your bed!

Do you understand?"

she says.

I can fib.

It is fun.

I can fib

to anyone.

I fib to Dad.

I fib to Mom.

Fib, fib, fib.

Fun, fun, fun.

See me shrug.

Hear me fib.

"But, Mom," I say,

"I never did.

It was not me.

It was my legs.

My naughty, wicked,

jumping legs."

See my mommy
shake her head.
See her drag me
off the bed.
Hear her say:
"That is not true.
I will have to
punish you."

See me struggle.

See me fight.

See my mommy

hold me tight.

Being punished

is not fun.

See me bite her.

See me run.

166

See me run.

Run, run, run.

See Mom run.

Run, run, run.

See us run.

Run, run, run.

Run, run, run.

Fun, fun, fun.

Around the bedroom.

Out the door.

See the staircase!

See me fall!

Down the stairs

on my rump.

Hear me bounce.

Bump, bump, bump.

See me land.

On the floor.

See me run.

To the door.

I must get out.

I must go fast.

Mom is looking

dangerous.

See the door.

It opens wide.

See two big legs.

They step inside.

This is not good.

This is bad.

Those big legs

belong to Dad.

I must get out.

I must get past.

I must think quick.

I must think fast.

I know what!

I'll play a game.

Dad's a tunnel.

And I'm a train!

"Look out!" I say.

"Let me through!

I'm a train.

Choo, choo, choo."

I push my head

against his knees.

"Toot-toot," I say.

"Open, please."

See Daddy smile.

He bends down low.

"Go, little train.

Go, go, go."

He opens his legs.

I'm almost out.

But then I hear

my mommy shout:

"Stop that boy!

Stop him now!

He must be stopped!

I don't care how!

He's jumped

and fibbed

and fought and bit.

He must not get

away with it!"

Feel Daddy's legs

squeeze me tight.

"What's this?" he says.

"This is not right!

You should not jump.

You should not fight.

You should not fib.

You should not bite."

See Daddy grab me
by the ear.

Hear Mommy whoop
and clap and cheer.

Hear Daddy rant, roar,
rave, and boom.

See them shut me
in my room.

BLAP!

OK
LET'S
GET
ORGANIZED

176

I'm in trouble.

I've been bad.

I sit on my bed.

I feel SAD.

But I know how

to make SAD stop.

I can jump.

I can hop.

Hop, hop, hop.

Jump, jump, jump.

Bounce, bounce, bounce.

Bump, bump, bump.

On my tummy.

On my bum.

See me jump.

Fun, fun, fun.

MUDMEN

I'm naked.

I'm shivering.

I'm banging on the back door as hard as I can.

"Dad!" I yell. "Dad! Let me in!"

I grab the door handle and push down with all my strength, but it's no use.

I must have forgotten to put the safety catch on the dead bolt. Now what? There's no other way into the house. All the windows are barred, and the front door has an even more foolproof dead bolt than the back door.

It's not my fault I'm out here with no clothes on.

It's Sooty's fault. He's gone crazy.

I came out to get my school uniform off the

clothesline, but it wasn't on the clothesline. It was all over the backyard. In shreds. The shreds were covered in mud — and so was Sooty. And while I was yelling at him, he stole the towel I had around my waist, ran under the porch, and started ripping it to shreds as well. I'd rip him to shreds if I was small enough to get under there.

"Dad!" I yell. "Please open the door! I'm freezing!"

Stupid Dad and his stupid dead bolts.

Ever since our house got broken into a few months ago, he's gone home-security crazy. You name it, we've got it — dead bolts, bars across the windows, a closed-circuit TV surveillance system, infrared motion detectors, and a fully monitored alarm system. Not to mention a Neighborhood Watch sticker on the mailbox.

It's a great system. Dad lost the keys yesterday morning and we were trapped inside for two hours. Mom and Jen are in Mildura for the week visiting my grandparents, so they couldn't help us. We had to wait until the police arrived, alerted by the alarm system.

"DAD!"

I yell even louder and bang on the door at the same time. But it's no use. He must still be in the shower. I'm going to have to go around to the bathroom window.

I go back down the steps and around the side of the house to the bathroom.

That's weird. I can't hear the shower running.

"Dad?" I call. "Are you in there?"

He doesn't answer.

"Dad?" I call again.

"Andy?" he calls. But not from the bathroom. He's calling from around the back of the house. He must have heard me the first time. I run along the side of the house and around to the backyard. Dad's standing outside the back door, a towel around his waist.

"What are you doing?" he says. "You're supposed to be getting ready for school — not wandering naked around the backyard!"

"It's not my fault," I say. "I *was* getting ready. I came outside to get my clothes off the line, but Sooty ripped them up and then he stole my towel. And then I couldn't get back inside because your dead bolts kept me out."

Dad sucks in his breath and begins to shake his head.

"It's always somebody else's fault, isn't it?" he says. "When are you going to start taking some responsibility for your own behavior?"

EXCUSES FOR NOT GOING TO SCHOOL.

MY DOG ATE MY CLOTHES.

MY MOTHER ATE MY CLOTHES.

MY PARENTS ATE ME.

I ATE MY PARENTS.

KNOCK KNOCK

"But it's true!" I say. "Sooty's gone crazy!"

"Now listen here," says Dad. "Let's get some things straight. Sooty is not crazy. . . ."

But while he is talking, Sooty emerges from underneath the porch.

"Dad!" I say.

"Don't interrupt me!" he says. "Second, it is not my fault if you get locked out of the house. I've explained how to use the dead bolts. . . ."

"Dad!" I say. "Look behind you!"

"I said don't interrupt me and I meant it!" says Dad, frowning.

"But," I say, watching Sooty get closer and closer to him. He's taking slow deliberate steps like he's stalking prey.

"Not another word!" says Dad.

Sooty strikes.

He leaps through the air, and in one deft movement rips Dad's towel from around his waist.

"What the . . . ?" says Dad.

He turns around, only to see Sooty disappearing underneath the porch with his towel.

Dad is standing there, nude, his mouth gaping.

"I hate to say I told you so," I say. "I mean,

182

I really, really, really hate to say I told you so, but I . . ."

"Shut up, Andy!" says Dad. "This is all your fault!"

"My fault?" I say. "But what about accepting responsibility for your own behavior?"

But Dad seems to have lost interest in that subject.

"Just come back inside, get dressed, and get ready for school," he says.

MR BAINBRIDGE IS FIT TO BE TIED.

"But what am I going to wear?" I say.

"One of your sister's dresses for all I care!" he says. "I just don't want to be late for work again. Mr. Bainbridge was fit to be tied yesterday."

(FROM PG. 151)
DR. WOMKLE'S DREAM DE-NEBULIZER.

Dad stomps back up the steps.

"What about the door?" I say. "Did you put the dead bolt safety catch on?"

"Of course I did," says Dad. "Think I don't know how to work a simple dead bolt?"

FREE HOME TRIAL? HUH!
IN YOUR DREAMS!!

He pushes down on the handle.

Nothing happens.

He tries it again. Still nothing.

He bangs his head against the door.

"Why me?" he says.

Bang.

"Why me?"

KNOCK. KNOCK.

183

THE MALE VACUUM.

IN THE MATING SEASON THE BULL VACUUM BECOMES VERY ACTIVE, WAVING HIS NOZZLE ABOUT AND RETRACTING HIS CORD FREQUENTLY.

FOR MORE VACUUM FACTS SEE PG: 38

Bang.

"What did I do to deserve this?"

Bang.

I put my hand on his shoulder.

"Dad?" I say.

"What?" he says.

"Do you think you should be doing that to your head?" I say.

"What else is there to do?" he says.

"Um," I say. "Try to find another way in?"

"There is no other way in," he says. "The doors are double dead-bolted. The windows are barred. And even if we could pry the bars apart, the motion detectors would alert the police long before we could get in."

"Well, why don't we do that?" I say.

Dad snorts.

"Use your head, Andy!" he says. "We're naked. We have no way of proving who we are. They'd arrest us."

"We could get the neighbors to vouch for us," I say. "They'd tell the police who we are."

Dad stops and thinks for a moment. Then he shakes his head.

"No," he says. "It's bad enough to be locked out of your own home, let alone having to pa-

184

AHEM

rade around nude in front of the neighbors. I'd be a laughingstock."

Hmmm. He's right. I don't exactly like the idea of being nude in front of the neighbors — not to mention the police — any more than Dad does. It's bad enough being nude in front of my dad, and even worse, to have him nude in front of me.

JANE
WAITS
FOR A BUS.

Then I have a brainstorm.

"What about the spare key?" I ask.

Dad moans. "It used to be under the doormat, but Neighborhood Watch says you shouldn't keep keys in such obvious places."

"So where is it now?" I say.

Dad moans again.

"I left it at work," he says. "In my office."

"We could go get it," I say.

"But we have no clothes on," says Dad.

Dad has a point. But we've got to do something. I'm freezing.

I jog up and down to try and keep warm. But I slip on the wet ground and fall backward onto the muddy lawn.

I get up.

My legs are covered in mud and little pieces of grass.

POKE!

Hey! I've got it.

"Dad," I say, "I know how we can get to your work and get the key!"

"How?" he says.

"We can cover ourselves in mud and grass. It will be like camouflage."

"Don't be stupid," says Dad. "This is serious."

"I'm not being stupid," I say. "Watch this!"

I scoop up a big double handful of mud and smear it across my chest. I grab another handful and rub it onto my belly. I lie down on my back and roll around until I'm completely covered — from head to toe — in mud.

All the while, Dad is standing there studying me like I'm something that just arrived from another planet.

"Well," I say. "What do you think?"

"I think you're completely insane," says Dad.

"Yes," I say, "I know, but we'd only have to travel a few blocks. If we stay in backyards wherever possible and move really fast across the open areas, we'll be there in no time and nobody will even notice us. It's still pretty early."

"It's a crazy plan," he says. "But . . ."

OUCH!

SORRY.

"But, Dad . . ." I say.

"Let me finish," he says. "I was going to say it's so crazy it just might work. Besides, I don't know what else we can do."

"Good point! I say. "What have we got to lose?"

"You're right," he says. "Let's do it!"

He bends down and starts slopping big handfuls of mud onto himself. He breaks into a broad grin.

"Well," he says, "how do I look?"

"Looking good, Dad!" I say. "Just like a regular mudman!"

The more mud he slops on, the more excited he gets. He's like a little kid. He pastes mud all over his body and all over his head. It's in his hair, his eyes, his mouth. He looks really freaky — not like my dad at all. He covers his private parts with a leaf and hands one to me.

"Better put this on," he says. "Just in case."

"Just in case what?" I say.

"In case somebody sees us," he says.

"Nobody will see us!" I say. "Because we're mudmen! Invisible to the eye! We travel where we want! When we want! How we want!"

"Mudmen!" says Dad, holding out his muddy hand, palm upward. "Give me five!"

TYPES OF LEAVES FOR COVERING YOUR PRIVATE PARTS.

1.

2.

3.

4.

5.

6.

IDIOT!

I give him five. Mud splashes out from our hands. I haven't seen Dad this excited since . . . since . . . well, actually I've never seen him this excited.

The sky is filled with dark clouds. That's good. It makes it less likely that we'll be seen.

We climb up our fence and into Mr. Broadbent's yard. Crouching low, we run across the yard and climb over his fence.

"So far, so good!" says Dad as we run across the second yard and scale the next fence.

We drop down into the third backyard. There's plenty of cover here. It's full of trees and shrubs.

"Too easy!" giggles Dad.

"See, I told you!" I say.

We continue on our way, leaping fences like they're nothing more than hurdles in a hundred-yard dash.

Wooden fences, chain-link fences, high-security fences — nothing stops us. We're mudmen!

We thread our way through compost heaps, swimming pools, and vegetable gardens. All the while getting more and more caked in mud and leaves and dirt.

188

We stop, panting, in the last backyard on our street.

"I haven't had this much fun since I was in the Boy Scouts!" says Dad, wheezing.

"You covered yourselves in mud and ran around the streets in Boy Scouts?" I say.

"No," he laughs. "We went hiking and orienteering — but this is much better!"

"Okay," I say. "We're going to have to run along the side of this house and cross the road to the house on the other side to get to the next set of backyards. Are you ready?"

"Ready!" says Dad.

We run down the side of the house and cross the sidewalk to the median strip.

Oh no!

There's a car coming out of the driveway of the house beside us.

There's no time to hide.

"What do we do now?" says Dad.

"Freeze!" I say. "Put your hands out to your side. We'll pretend we're trees!"

We both stop dead and put our arms out at weird angles.

"I don't think we look much like trees," whispers Dad out of the side of his mouth.

REX STROMSKI'S WALK TO WORK NAKED BACKWARD!

189

He's right, but it doesn't seem to matter.

The driver of the car doesn't even give us a second glance as he pulls out onto the road and takes off.

"Phew, that was close," says Dad.

"But we did it!" I say.

"Yeah!" he says, his muddy eyes shining. "We did it!"

He runs across the road and leaps over the low brick fence that runs along the front of the house on the corner. I follow him, along the side of the house, into the backyard, and over the fence.

Dad's really moving now. I have to run as fast as I can to keep up with him.

As I'm climbing over a tall green fence I see him standing under a clothesline in the middle of a yard. He's holding a large pair of jeans above his head. I drop down into the yard and join him.

"Look what I found!" he says. "This should make things easier!"

"Great, Dad," I say. "But let's keep moving. Before someone sees us."

Dad is bending over, trying to put on the jeans.

190

Out of the corner of my eye, I notice something move.

I hear growling.

Uh-oh.

I quickly review how many yards we've been through and I realize what backyard we're in . . . the backyard of number 19. The home of the pit bull.

It comes running across the grass toward Dad.

"Forget the jeans, Dad," I say. "Run!"

I head toward the fence. The pit bull follows me, baring its teeth and snarling. I start climbing the fence, the pit bull snapping at my legs.

Dad runs toward us. He twirls the jeans around and flicks them like they're a rolled-up dish towel. He hits the dog on its back. It turns and attacks him.

Dad grabs the pit bull around the stomach and wrestles it to the ground. They roll around together in the mud. Fighting, thrashing, and growling. It's hard to tell who's growling the loudest. It's incredible. I've never seen Dad like this before. It's like watching Tarzan wrestle a leopard.

Dad looks up at me.

THERE
ARE NO
DRAWINGS
ON THIS
PAGE.

"What are you waiting for?" he yells. "Go!"

But I can't. I can't tear myself away. The pit bull is winning. It's on top of Dad, its fangs bared, ready to sink them into Dad's neck.

"No!" I scream.

IT IS
NAKED!

But then in one amazingly fast movement, Dad reaches up, grabs the dog's neck, clamps its jaws shut with his hand and wraps the jeans around its muzzle and head. He ties the legs of the jeans in a knot and pulls them tight.

Dad leaps up onto the fence and swings his legs over onto the other side. The dog is staggering around the backyard, blinded by the jeans, furiously trying to shake them off its head. It crashes into a tree and falls over.

I drop down and join Dad.

(OR WOULD
BE IF THIS
WRITING
EXPLAINING
THAT IT IS
NAKED
WASN'T
HERE.)

"That was amazing, Dad!" I say. "Too bad you had to give up your jeans, though."

Dad is wired, electric, alive.

"Doesn't matter," he says, beaming. "What do I need with jeans, anyway? I'm a MUD-MAN!"

Mudman? He looks more like a madman. His hair's all stiff with mud and sticking out at crazy angles. His eyes are wide and white and he's got blood dripping from a wound on his shoulder where the pit bull bit him. He looks wild.

IRON-GLOVE WHO?

"Come on," he says. "We've got to keep moving."

I can't believe how much Dad's gotten into this. It's like he's not even my dad anymore.

We make it through the next five backyards without any problems. We jump over the last fence into an alley.

"Not far now!" says Dad.

We sprint down the alley as fast as we can. At the end of the alley, we flatten our backs against a wall. We look out across a busy highway. The traffic is bumper-to-bumper.

Dad's work is on the other side of the road. There is a factory, a warehouse, and a two-story office building. Dad's office is on the second floor.

"We're almost there," says Dad. "All we have to do is cross the road."

"Hang on," I say. "Just one question. How do we get to your office? We can't exactly go through reception."

"But we're mudmen!" he says. "We can go anywhere we want!"

"But not through reception," I say. "Think about it."

Dad thinks.

"You're right," he says. "Mrs. Lewis might have a heart attack."

WATER-
MELON

NAKED
WATER-
MELON.

193

NOT IRON-GLOVE!
EYE AND GLOVE!

We stand in the alley and study the buildings.

We're so close, and yet, so far.

I really thought we were going to make it.

It's hard to believe that we've come all this way for nothing.

Suddenly, Dad grabs my arm.

"I've got it!" he says. "See that shed near the fence?" He points to a small gray building just inside the gate.

I nod.

"What about it?" I say.

"It's a maintenance shed," he says. "They keep overalls in there. We can put them on and go and get the key. No problem. No heart attacks. Let's go."

The cars are still bumper-to-bumper.

"Hang on," I say. "Are we just going to run across the road? Shouldn't we wait until there's a break in the traffic?"

"It'll be like this for another hour, at least," says Dad. "We haven't got time. Just keep your eyes straight ahead and don't look back!"

I look at him.

He pats me on the back.

"Come on, mudboy," he says. "You can do it."

THE ANTI-
NAKEDNESS
COMMITTEE
"PANTS ON"
CAMPAIGN.
↓

BOOKS.

ART.

TRANSPORT.

MEDIA.

WHAT?

194

EYE.
GLOVE.

I put my hands up on either side of my face like blinkers. If I can't see them, they can't see me.

We thread our way through the cars.

People are yelling and hooting and honking their horns.

They've obviously never seen mudmen before.

Dad is just in front of me, moving quickly through the traffic. We come to an SUV that's so close to the car in front we can't get through. Dad leaps over the hood in one bound. I take my hands away from my face and follow him.

"Andy?" says a voice, as I climb across the front of the car.

I look at the driver.

Oh no.

It's my teacher, Ms. Livingstone.

"Hi," I say. "I know this looks a little strange, but . . ."

She raises her hand and smiles.

"Not to me," she says. "I spent six months living with mudpeople and I'll never forget it. There was this one time . . ."

Uh-oh. Ms. Livingstone's travel stories are fascinating, but once she gets started, she can go on for hours.

MS. LIVINGSTONE'S NEW FLAT HEAD.

BLAH BLAH BLAH

SKLITCHH!

HUH?

195

A NAKED MECHANICAL CHICKEN.
↓

"I'd love to hear about it sometime, Ms. Livingstone," I say, "but I'm kind of in a hurry right now."

She smiles and nods.

"I understand," she says. "That's exactly how the mudpeople were — never still, always rushing here and there. I remember one time . . ."

I slide off the hood and keep running.

We reach the other side of the road and sprint along the fence to the front gates of Dad's work.

There's nobody around. That's good.

We cut across to the maintenance shed.

Dad tries to open the door.

It's locked. That's bad.

"Darn!" says Dad, slamming his fist on the door. "The caretaker usually has this unlocked by now."

He steps back from the door and looks at the shed.

"What are we going to do now?" he says. "We're doomed!"

"No we're not, Dad," I say. "We're mudmen, remember? We can do anything!"

"We're not mudmen," he says. "We're just a couple of naked morons covered in mud. I

MUDMEN. FIRST PEOPLE TO CLIMB MT. EVEREST NAKED. (EXCEPT FOR THIN LAYER OF MUD.)

EYE. GLOVE
EYE GLOVE

should have known this wouldn't work. I should never have listened to you. What on earth was I thinking?"

I look at Dad. Something has changed. A few minutes ago he was running through the streets without his clothes on, leaping over cars and fences, and fighting dogs with his bare hands. Now he's staring at me with wide desperate eyes. I have to take over.

I turn away from Dad and study the shed. There's a set of windows above the door.

"Maybe I can get in through there," I say. "I could slide out the glass and climb through."

"But how are you going to get up there?" says Dad.

"On your shoulders," I say. "Crouch down."

Dad crouches and looks around nervously.

"Okay," he says. "But hurry. People will be arriving any minute now."

I put one foot on his mud-caked shoulders. The mud is half dried and gives my foot plenty of grip. I grab Dad's right hand and pull myself up onto his other shoulder. I grab his left hand and steady myself.

"Okay," I say. "I'm ready."

Dad stands up and I rise up to the level of the window.

I WOULD LIKE TO SEE MORE NAKEDNESS IN THIS STORY.

ME, TOO

EYE GLOVE YOU, TOO

197

I let go of his hand and try to remove the first pane of glass. It's not easy, though. It won't budge. I try to loosen it by rattling it and it moves a little, but not much.

"I can't open it," I call down to Dad. "It's stuck."

"Try the next one up," he says. "Hurry!"

I try it. Much better. It slides out smoothly. I place the glass on the gutter above me and start to work on the next one. It slides out easily, too.

I go back to the first window.

It's still stuck.

I feel a drop of water on my head.

And another.

I look up.

Uh-oh. It's starting to rain.

Just what we didn't need.

There is an enormous clap of thunder. The clouds open up suddenly and the first few drops give way to the most incredible downpour. It's like the cloud above us has been holding on for weeks, months — possibly years. But not anymore. Down it comes. Right on top of us. On top of our mud. And begins to wash it away.

"Hurry up, Andy!" says Dad.

I OBJECT TO THE CONSTANT AND UNNECESSARY USE OF NAKEDNESS IN THIS STORY. IT'S JUST WACKY!

198

I'VE ALWAYS GLOVED YOU. WELCOME HOME.

"I'm trying to!" I yell, "but the window is stuck."

"Just break it!" pleads Dad. "I'll replace it later! We have to get those overalls!"

I can hardly see anything. The mud is washing off my hair and into my eyes. It must be even worse for Dad because all my mud is washing off me and down onto him. I wipe my eyes and try to figure out how to break the window.

I'm just about to karate-chop it when I hear a noise. A car is pulling up alongside us.

I look over my shoulder.

Uh-oh.

It's Mr. Bainbridge. Dad's boss.

He's getting out of the passenger side of the car.

The car is being driven by Mrs. Bainbridge.

"Andy?" says Mr. Bainbridge.

"Who is that?" says Dad, turning around to see.

"No!" I scream. "Don't turn around!"

But it's too late.

I teeter on his shoulders as he turns. Dad puts his hands up to steady me. I grab them.

"*Aagghh!*" says Mr. Bainbridge.

199

"Aagghh!" says Dad.

"Cover your eyes, dear!" yells Mr. Bainbridge, running around to the driver's side of the car to stand in front of Mrs. Bainbridge's window.

MR. BAINBRIDGE SUDDENLY REALIZES HE HAS TURNED UP TO WORK NAKED.

BUT IT IS NOT WORLD GO-TO-WORK-NAKED DAY.

Now don't get me wrong, but I'm not too worried about the Bainbridges seeing *me* in the nude. It's happened so many times now that it's almost routine, but I feel for Dad. This is his first time ever.

"So this is where he gets it from," says Mr. Brainbridge. "Like father, like son!"

"I'm very sorry, Mr. Bainbridge," says Dad. "I know this seems highly irregular, but I can assure you there is a very good reason. . . ."

Mr. Bainbridge puts up his hand.

"Don't waste my time and your breath," he says. "As you well know, I am a man of high standards, and I demand the same from my employees. I do not expect to come to work and find them naked, covered in mud, and performing acrobatics in the driveway. I've come to expect this sort of behavior from your feral son, but for a man of your age and in your position, it is inexcusable! I will not tolerate it. You are fired."

200

"But Mr. Bainbridge," splutters Dad. "I . . . I . . . I . . ."

Poor Dad. He's struggling here. He's obviously not as used to making up excuses as I am.

"It's okay, Dad," I say. "I'll handle this."

I look down at Mr. Bainbridge.

"You can't fire my dad!" I say.

"And why not?" says Mr. Bainbridge.

"Because this isn't really happening," I say.

"Not happening?" says Mr. Bainbridge. "What are you talking about?"

"It's a hallucination," I say. "You've been working very hard lately. We're just products of your confused mind. You should get back in the car, go home, and have a good long nap . . ."

"That'll do, Andy," says Dad.

"Don't listen to him, Mr. Bainbridge," I yell. "He's a hallucination. He doesn't know what he's talking about."

"No, Andy," says Dad, "no more lies."

Dad bends down and lowers me to the ground. He stands up straight and faces Mr. Bainbridge.

"Mr. Bainbridge," he says, "I don't mind at all that you've fired me because you've just saved me the trouble of quitting."

201

Mr. Bainbridge gasps in shock. So do I. And so does Mrs. Bainbridge, who is peeking out from behind Mr. Bainbridge.

"You see," says Dad, "I realized something about myself this morning. I realized that I've been living a half-life. A safe life. A boring life. A life of too much responsibility and not enough fun. Not enough danger."

What is Dad talking about? Obviously, the stress of being locked out of his house without any clothes on has driven him over the edge.

WACKY FOR LIFE.

CHIRP

"Dad," I say, "do you know what you're saying? Are you crazy?"

"Yes," says Dad, putting his arm around my shoulders. "I'm crazy all right. Crazy for life! I want to take more chances, climb more mountains, swim more rivers, and watch more sunsets. Life's too short to waste, Andy. You, me, Mom, and Jen — we're going to escape this rat race. We're going to leave the city. We're going to live off the land — in the wild — in the raw."

"We are?!" I say.

"Yes," says Dad, sweeping his arm through the air. "We don't need all . . . this! Come on, son, let's get out of here."

"But, Dad," I say, "what about the overalls?"

Dad kneels down and picks up a fresh handful of mud and starts slapping it all over himself.

"Overalls?" he says. "Who needs overalls when we've got mud?"

"But the key," I say. "We haven't got the key."

"We don't need a key," he says. "We'll climb onto the roof and go down the chimney like we should have done in the first place! It'll be a challenge. And, more important, it will be fun!"

He slaps a few more handfuls of mud carelessly across his body and marches off down the driveway, not even looking back.

It's stopped raining. The clouds have broken up and golden rays of light illuminate my dad, highlighting every muscle in his body. He looks stronger than I ever imagined he could.

Mr. and Mrs. Bainbridge are just staring, slack-jawed.

I give them a shrug and run after my dad.

Well, what else can I do?

I'm a little worried about how our new life is going to work exactly, and what Mom and Jen are going to think about it when they get back home, but speaking for myself, I think it sounds kind of fun.

Wacky, but fun.

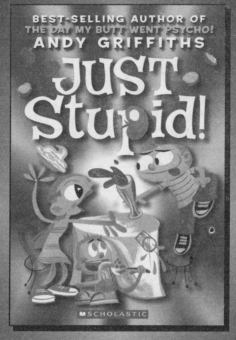

How disgusting can you get?

THEY'VE BEEN SMACKED, PINCHED,

KICKED, AND SAT ON.

AND THEY'RE FUMING MAD!

BEST-SELLING AUTHOR
ANDY GRIFFITHS

THE DAY MY BUTT WENT PSYCHO!

BASED ON A TRUE STORY

SCHOLASTIC

THE *New York Times* BESTSELLER!

PLAY THE MOVE YOUR BUTT GAME AT
WWW.SCHOLASTIC.COM/PSYCHOBUTT

SCHOLASTIC

DMBWPT

LOOK WHAT'S JUST LANDED!

THE SEQUEL TO ANDY GRIFFITHS'S NEW YORK TIMES BESTSELLER THE DAY MY BUTT WENT PSYCHO!

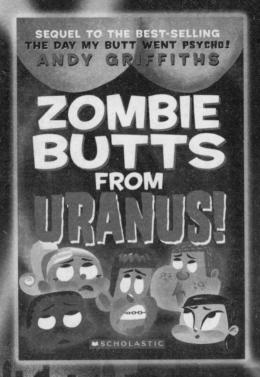

IN THIS HEART-STOPPING, NOSTRIL-BURNING INTERGALACTIC ADVENTURE, YOUNG ZACK MUST STOP AN INVASION OF ZOMBIE BUTTS FROM TAKING OVER THE PLANET. CAN OUR DOODY-FULL HERO STAND UP TO THESE STENCH INVADERS —OR WILL HE CRACK? THE GALAXY IS BUT ONE BOY (AND HIS BUTT) AWAY FROM TOTAL REEK-DOM.

SCHOLASTIC

WWW.SCHOLASTIC.COM/ANDYGRIFFITHS

About the Author

Andy Griffiths discovered a talent for wacky behavior after accidentally sitting on an ants' nest. Since then, he has alarmed the world with even wackier antics, including sitting on an ants' nest in the nude, sitting on a nude ants' nest, and letting nude ants sit on him. He has written four other titles in the JUST series, as well as two extremely wacky bestselling novels — *The Day My Butt Went Psycho!* and *Zombie Butts from Uranus!* — and has accidentally destroyed the universe and every living creature in it on at least three separate occasions.

About the Illustrator

Terry Denton is an illustrator. He gets to illustrate a lot. He is lucky. Luckier than if he were a builder. If he were a builder, he would hardly get to illustrate at all. If he were a dog, same thing . . . not much illustration. He has a friend who makes plastic things that fit on the ends of hoses. That friend doesn't get to illustrate at all. Not that he minds, because he loves making plastic things that fit on the ends of hoses. He'd hate to be an illustrator. Terry, however, would hate to make plastic things that fit on the ends of hoses. That's why he is an illustrator.